JEWELS BENEATH THE LOCH

The Descendants of Gods

Book Two

By: R.M. Alwyn

CONTENTS

Prologue

Chapter 1: The Glitter Path

Chapter 2: The Seeds of the Future

Chapter 3: The Quad Squad

Chapter 4: Crystal Gardens

Chapter 5: A Paradoxical Beauty

Chapter 6: The Worshippers

Chapter 7: True Calling

Chapter 8: The Crocodile's Resurgence

Chapter 9: Neighborhood Watch

Chapter 10: The Wolf God

Chapter 11: Destiny Unfolds

Chapter 12: Medical Miracles

Chapter 13: Tragedy in Bali

Chapter 14: The Scourge of Warriors

Chapter 15: A Clash of Cultures

Chapter 16: The Disconcerting Text

Chapter 17: Cruel Deception

Chapter 18: Environmental Soldiers

Chapter 19: The Blacksmith Killer

Chapter 20: Global Pandemic

Chapter 21: The Changing Tides

Chapter 22: The White Bear Goddess

Chapter 23: The Mistress of Revelry

Chapter 24: Conflicting Approaches

Chapter 25: Harbingers of Bad Fortune

Chapter 26: Bewildering Transformations

Chapter 27: The Search for Lost Love

Chapter 28: The Plastic Future

Chapter 29: Hope for a Cure

Chapter 30: Seeking Acceptance

Chapter 31: The Medical Maverick

Chapter 32: The Haunted Mansion

Chapter 33: A Master Plan Unfolds

Chapter 34: A Village of Legends

Chapter 35: The Distress Signal

Chapter 36: Echoes of the Fortress

Chapter 37: London Calling

Chapter 38: A Menacing Revelation

Chapter 39: Heavenly Disco

Chapter 40: The Dragon Gallery

Chapter 41: Ancient Astrology

Chapter 42: A Beautiful Reunion

Chapter 43: The Ancestral Spirits

Chapter 44: The Journey North

Chapter 45: The Homecoming

Chapter 46: Vials of Hate

Chapter 47: A Lost Soul

Chapter 48: Underwater Warriors

Chapter 49: Prelude to Havoc

Chapter 50: The Gathering Storm

Chapter 51: Smash and Grab

Chapter 52: Unseen by Mortals

Chapter 53: Beneath the Moonlight and beyond the Grave

Chapter 54: The Fiery Crucible

Chapter 55: Facing the Dark Depths

Chapter 56: Rescue is Imminent

Chapter 57: Awe and Trepidation

Chapter 58: Guardians of the Treasury

Chapter 59: Chaotic Waters

Chapter 60: The Battle Resumes

Chapter 61: Smoke Rises

Chapter 62: Returning to Normal

PROLOGUE

Drifting beneath a majestic mist, where heather dusted landscapes harbor ancient mysteries, a realm steeped in Celtic lore beckons.

Spirits ride the whispering winds while shapeshifters morph among trees. Brownies, fairies, and goblins dance in the water's silver reflections. Their ethereal presence stirs an unspoken harmony within the faithful, touching the depths of the soul.

As sacred groves turn into gateways to the heavens, curious phantoms are invited to traverse the boundary between the tangible and the unseen. Each hill, stone and mirrored loch resonates with a unique essence, revealing the deep connection between the physical and spiritual worlds.

Here in the Scottish Highlands, ancient runes embrace the tendrils of aged vines, bridging human history and folklore.

CHAPTER 1

THE GLITTER PATH

Darren Surch lived in a modest farmhouse nestled at the edge of a vibrant green meadow overlooking Loch Ness. Shielded from the fierce winds that swept in from the Moray Firth and North Sea by a thicket of protective trees, his home found solace under grand Scots Pines and silver birches that encircled three magnificent oak trees. These towering sentinels offered their strength and support to the humble dwelling. A few miles away from the picturesque village of Drumnadrochit the aptly named Triple Tree Farm stood on the road to Inverness. Darren's ancestral crofter's house, built over a century ago in 1710 by his great-grandfather, stood resilient despite its near destruction by the English during the turbulent Jacobite rebellion.

Undeterred by adversity, Darren's family had rebuilt the house with fortified double walls filled with earth, providing insulation against the harsh Scottish winter.

The timber roof, thatched with reeds and grass from the loch, offered protection from the elements, allowing snow to elegantly slide off during winter. Inside, stone slabs laid out on the floor encircled a central fireplace and chimney that skillfully guided the smoke from the peat fire out into the brisk Scottish air. The crackling fire and flickering candles combined to envelop the home in a snug and welcoming warmth, casting a comforting glow throughout the house.

Darren cared for his herd of cattle that included Shaggy Highland cows, Aberdeen Angus, and Limousin breeds.

Additionally, he reared a few sheep and pigs to supplement his income. Labor was scarce due to the decimation of the Jacobite army at the Battle of Culloden Moor, leaving many young men fallen. Despite receiving limited help since those dark times from his wife and young son, Darren faced the challenge of the farm's upkeep virtually alone.

However, Darren's current preoccupation lay with the perplexing disappearance of one cow and two sheep from his property. He suspected it to be the work of rustlers from Inverness. Vowing to capture these cunning culprits who resorted to stealing and selling the fruits of his labor to complicit butchers in the city, Darren armed himself with his grandfather's basket-hilted broadsword, a trusted targe shield, and a dirk. Taking a strategic position near the road from Inverness, he kept a watchful eye not only on his land and livestock but also on the dark waters of the Loch.

Regardless of the season, Loch Ness held an air of mystery with its ominous black hue, a result of peat sediment flowing down from the surrounding hills. Each glimmer of light on its surface mirrored the stars in the night sky, creating an enchanting sight.

As the moon ascended casting its radiant glow over the loch, a mesmerizing spectacle unfolded. A luminous "glitter path" shimmered like liquid stardust. Time crept by as Darren fought to keep his concentration on the winding road ahead. The frigid air wrapped around him like icy fingers, tempting him with visions of his cozy bed. Yet, his determination to apprehend the rustlers spurred him on.

Suddenly, an abrupt flicker of movement caught his peripheral vision, stirring a sense of intrigue, as ripples danced on the surface the water. Bathed in the moonlight, a colossal and enigmatic creature appeared from the depths of the loch. Gliding gracefully with the elegance of a titanic serpent, the creature's gargantuan oval-shaped head gleamed like crude oil. It cast an eerie reflection, while its deep-set obsidian eyes added to its powerful allure. In a fleeting moment, the mysterious creature moved through the water with otherworldly grace, its two distinct humps creating a mesmerizing sight.

Captivated by its elegant motion, Darren watched as the shadowy ribbon danced in the moonlight. Suddenly, it darted towards the heart of the loch and swiftly disappeared. He stood open-mouthed and awestruck as he watched the creature vanish into the murky depths.

Intrigued, Darren felt compelled to touch the gentle ripples left in the monster's wake as they kissed the shore. Under the shroud of night, a serene tranquility enveloped the valley, and the gentle melody of the wind whispered through the reeds. The moonlight bathed the grass in a silvery sheen, its silent sway in harmony as Darren stood, lost in contemplation. The icy water running through his fingers jolted him back into reality. A sense of wonder gripped him, pondering whether this enigmatic creature held the key to the mystery of his missing livestock.

Doubt's shadows deepened, dancing at the edges of his mind.

CHAPTER 2

THE SEEDS OF THE FUTURE

Ten thousand years ago, amidst the vast expanse of space, a catastrophic event unfolded, shattering the tranquil interstellar journey of the Izbek. Their once majestic ship now bore scars from a collision with a malevolent shard of space debris, leaving them paralyzed and adrift. Peering through the cracked viewports of their wounded vessel, the Izbek beheld a mesmerizing spectacle of celestial wonders. Swirling nebulas and distant galaxies danced along their silvery-mirrored fuselage, a stark contrast to the gaping scar marring their once-proud hull.

An undercurrent of uncertainty swirled, heightening their fears as they teetered on the edge of annihilation. their existence was hanging by a thread.

As the damaged ship spun in a perilous orbit towards the menacing black hole at the heart of the Milky Way, the Izbek's gaze fell upon a distant blue-green planet. A flicker of hope appeared when they were able to gain minimal control and steer their crippled vessel towards this oasis.

The radiant landscape below captured their weary hearts. It offered a potential sanctuary for survival. United by desperation and resilience, the Izbek faced a harsh reality.

The cold expanse of space had claimed many of their kin, leaving them with mourning eyes and ears that echoed with the anguished cries of their comrades. The somber truth settled upon them; not all could attempt the journey home. Some would have to stay on the planet below and await a rescue ship that might never arrive.

Yet in the face of despair, the Izbek rallied their strength.

Fueled by the will to survive, they forged a bond with the enigmatic blue planet.

Gifted with shapeshifting abilities, they could blend in and navigate the harsh terrains that awaited. Above the nascent world as they repaired their crippled vessel, the Izbek planted seeds of hope.

They jettisoned pulsating energy crystals that scattered across the unforgiving landscapes of icy peaks, shimmering glaciers, and polar wastelands. These crystals, once harvested and channeled through their mystical amulets, would grant them strength and dominion.

Departing in shimmering escape pods mirroring silver raindrops descending from the sky, the Izbek to be marooned bid farewell to their old vessel as it faded into the distance.

Reshaping their destiny, the castaways thrived, leaving an indelible mark on the evolving inhabitants of Earth.

Since their arrival, the advanced technology of the Izbek elevated them above all creatures, including humans. They ushered in a new era of civilization and prosperity.

However, as time passed, their influence waned but humanity continued to flourish, forcing the Izbek to skillfully navigate the shifting currents of belief and power.

Cloaked in secrecy, they shaped humanity from behind veils of mystery. They assumed varied roles throughout history.

Rising to positions of authority, they orchestrated the world's symphony, adapting to the ebb and flow of civilizations.

As time marched on, the Izbek entwined themselves in the human experience. Driven by primal desires, they sought companions and embraced parenthood. Some of their extraordinary offspring inherited their gifts, while many remained unaware of their lineage.

Yet, many people may have an inexplicable intuition and a connection to something beyond their comprehension. This phenomenon is common, as many individuals acknowledge a special affinity with animals, these connections etched deep in the fabric of their DNA—a heritage of mystery and intrigue.

CHAPTER 3

THE QUAD SQUAD

E ver since their encounter with the Izbek shapeshifters at Lake Mead, the Squad has grown immeasurably closer as a true team. Their Izbek ancestors shared ancient knowledge and gifted captivating amulets to them. Each member has an incredible array of abilities, enabling them to seamlessly transform into magnificent creatures of unparalleled prowess, drawing upon the strength of their Izbek ancestors.

Jose Aguilar, a young and adventurous spirit with an insatiable desire to soar through the sky like a bird, effortlessly assumes the form of a majestic eagle. His wings reach out, massaging the air as he gracefully glides above the breathtaking landscapes of Southern California. His eyes fill with wonderment, and his heart is aflame with a flyer's burning passion.

Sarah Sirent discovers pure delight and tranquility amidst the depths of the vast ocean. She undergoes a miraculous metamorphosis, bestowing upon her powerful fins and the sleek form of a playful dolphin. Filled with an irresistible zest for life, she weaves through the deep-blue waves.

Effortlessly embracing the feeling of absolute freedom, Sarah dances harmoniously with the rhythmic cadence of the Pacific

Ocean.

Under the full moon, Miles Cawtheray merges his very essence with the primordial energy that courses through the universe. He transforms into a formidable black panther.

Empowered with heightened senses and predatory elegance, he unearths a hidden wellspring of inner strength.

Lastly, Ichiro Kitzunaki personifies the essence of a fox: cunning, sly, and aloof. His transformation into this wily creature grants him unparalleled dexterity, agility and an elevated awareness of the world that enfolds him. He fluidly traverses the terrain, embracing the shadows that conceal his true intentions.

United by extraordinary, shared experiences, they have forged an unbreakable bond and call themselves the Quad Squad. During moments of introspection, the Squad articulates the profound sensations and intrinsic attributes that go with their exceptional transformations.

Yet despite their remarkable abilities, the Squad stays acutely aware of the delicate balance between keeping their shared humanity and embracing the immense potential of their powers. After meeting the ancestral Izbek and absorbing their profound wisdom, they have grown to understand that with great power comes great responsibility. They are determined to wield their exceptional talents for the greater good.

Together, they stand against the rogue Izbek who remain on Earth. individuals whose twisted desires consist of exploiting their shape-shifting abilities for their own purposes and orchestrating the demise of humanity. At the helm of this malevolent faction are Sobek and Wepwawet, power-hungry ancient extraterrestrials. Guided by their insatiable thirst for dominion, these castaways look to resurrect their empire's iron grip over humankind, much as they did in the days of yore in Mesopotamia and Ancient Egypt. Their nefarious plans involve harnessing the formidable power of alien crystalline energy, aiming to subjugate humanity while disrupting the natural course of its development. In doing so, they not only pose a significant threat to the world at large but also endanger the very fabric of existence itself.

Fresh from their most recent mission at the Hoover Dam, where the Squad uncovered the secrets concealed within a ten-thousand-year-old Izbek sphere hidden deep within a covert laboratory, they felt their understanding of their own origins deepen. The amulets, gifted to them by their Izbek progenitors, now allow them to summon lightning that crackles and dances between their fingertips. Guided by the ancient wisdom passed down by their space-traveling ancestors, the Squad wholeheartedly embraces their sacred duty to protect and defend the vulnerable.

CHAPTER 4

CRYSTAL GARDENS

Hovering above Earth, the spacecraft readied itself for the challenging journey home. The remaining crew gazed upon the shimmering beauty and extraordinary power of the crystals. These invaluable artifacts were to be jettisoned from the ship and positioned to aid their stranded brethren on the unfamiliar planet below. Thriving only in sub-zero temperatures, the crystals' energy would fade into the wind like ethereal whispers if the mercury climbed above freezing. Insulated chambers intricately crafted to nurture crystal growth, were placed at key locations on the planet's surface. These selected spots included the towering snow-capped peaks, the frost-coated expanses of the polar ice caps, and the mesmerizing electric-blue glaciers. Each chamber served as a cradle for the burgeoning crystals, aiding their evolution into reservoirs of power.

One of these crystal growth chambers found its home atop a towering glacier in the Scottish Highlands. Over time, as the glacier retreated, it revealed a hidden secret beneath its icy cloak. As the glacier succumbed to the passage of time, a majestic loch appeared, a testament to the vestiges of the frozen giant. Named Loch Ness, it possessed a mysterious depth seeming to extend to the very core of the Earth.

Within this enigmatic domain, concealed beneath the peaceful waters, the crystals found their sanctuary.

Resting on the lakebed shrouded in the dark waters of the Loch, the crystals settled where the temperature remained forever locked in an icy embrace. Here in a cryogenic realm, an ethereal garden of crystalline wonders took root.

Flourishing unabated by the loch's rippling currents, the crystals adorned the inky depths like celestial stars trapped beneath a mystical sea.

Across the ages, the crystals of Loch Ness grew into a source of vitality. If discovered, their radiant energy would empower any surviving castaways to endure their extended isolation. Retrieved from the depths, the castaways could harness the essence of these exquisite jewels and replenish the energy of their amulets. Even in proximity, their amulets would invigorate their wearers and equip them with newfound powers.

Here, within the depths of Loch Ness, the Izbek crew bestowed upon their stranded kin a lasting lifeline. They envisioned that the castaways would draw strength from the unyielding power of the crystals, nurturing hope within their hearts—that one day they would find their way back to their celestial home.

CHAPTER 5

A PARADOXICAL BEAUTY

I n a realm where celestial beauty intertwines with immense power, a being of awe-inspiring grace descends from the heavens above. The Culebre, a hermaphroditic dragon god, appears from a fiery egg—a vessel of divine creation hurled from the stars onto the surface of the earth. Its presence reminds mortals of the omnipotent force that birthed the very essence of creation.

As the Culebre unfurls its wings, a shimmering cascade of colors catches the eye, captivating any who dare to look.

Hypnotic amber eyes brimming with intelligence and compassion peer into the souls of those who pay reverence to the deity's magnificence. Within the depths of the mountain caves of Asturias, the Culebre carves its dwelling - a sanctuary of solitude and a haven of tranquility.

Sharp claws and webbed wings accentuate the dragon god's mighty form, while a resplendent head adorned with a vibrant array of feathers displays its otherworldly aesthetic.

Such paradoxical beauty emanates from its being. a representation of its non-binary nature, transcending traditional boundaries of gender. The Culebre is a testament to the exquisite balance found within the harmonious embrace of both masculine and feminine energies.

Wherever it roams the Culebre becomes elusive, enshrouding itself in smoke clouds and mist that billow gracefully in its wake. It is a shapeshifter of extraordinary prowess, seamlessly transforming into a breathtaking vision.

One that is neither man nor woman but handsome as well as strikingly beautiful. Such versatility embodies the fluidity of its divine essence, a celestial being unrestricted by the confines of a singular form.

Gently cradled within its palm, the Culebre carries a jewel of transcendent power, a purple Cintamani radiating with mystical energy. It is a reminder of the deity's extraordinary abilities, a conduit through which the extraordinary is made possible.

Among its kind, the Culebre was the ninth to descend from the skies. a number holding a profound significance.

Adorning its back are nine majestic ridges, each standing for a fragment of its divine lineage. Eighty-one scales glimmer with ancient wisdom, reminding those who bear witness of the sacred nature of its existence.

September holds sway over the Culebre's divine realm; the ninth month and one of transition and abundant life. As the protector of crops and the benefactor of agriculture, the dragon god harnesses its power to summon rain clouds during times of drought. With a voice that resonates through valleys, it calls upon the sun to caress the fields. ripening them to a bountiful harvest. Guiding humanity towards sustenance and prosperity, the Culebre's benevolence echoes in grain stalks that sway with the wind and every fruit tree that reaches for the sky.

In the very core of this being of dualistic beauty lies a wellspring of wonderment, power, and compassion. The Culebre, revered and respected as a guardian, is a symbol of the intricate tapestry that weaves together the celestial and earthly realms.

Scheduled as the ninth pod to be released from the mothership, they followed their life partner with whom they shared a profound emotional connection. An undeniable trepidation emanated from their amber eyes. Since their earliest days on Izbekia, the number nine had held deep significance in their life —a symbol of luck and importance.

Emerging from the vast sea after nine cycles of lunar interchanges, they had earned an impressive nine citations of merit during their coming-of-age ceremony. Taking a deep breath, echoing the release of air signaling the pod's departure, doubts lingered, questioning the decision to stay on this perilous planet. Yet, after consulting their soulmate, who reassured them that they would face the unknown together, they found comfort in their shapeshifting prowess—a unique ability that might prove helpful for their survival.

The pod settled on a slope that offered a mesmerizing view of a fertile valley and a meandering river flowing towards a vast sea. Towering mountains of granite teeth, dusted with a pristine layer of ethereal white, formed an impenetrable barrier behind them. The valley below captivated them, teeming with creatures they had never seen before. Grazing by the babbling waters and quenching their thirst from the river, these unknown beings sparked an insatiable curiosity.

Clutching their amulet tightly, they realized that neither their beloved partner nor any other Izbek were nearby, signaling that they would have to face the trials of survival alone. A wave of sadness and uncertainty washed over them. They wondered if they would ever be rescued.

With cautious intrigue, they kept a safe distance, silently observing the intricate tapestry of life unfolding in this new world. Among the inhabitants, two distinct bipedal species were competing for the abundant resources within the valley.

Seeking shelter, the castaway made their home in an expansive cave. Using the power of their amulet they transformed the cavern into a comfortable sanctuary reminiscent of their home on Izbekia. Within its depths, astonishing revelations awaited them—ancient paintings adorning the walls depicted animals, hunts, and a spectacular panorama of the night sky created by primitive primates.

Amidst these captivating artworks, a particular celestial beast caught their attention. Depicted as a winged creature conjured from blazing bonfires, they were unaware that this image originated from the imagination of ancient humanoids, recounting tales of immense creatures whose bones were unearthed along the riverbank. These humanoids experienced visions influenced by fermented and decaying fruits, with tendrils of smoke weaving fantastical tales in their minds.

Driven by insatiable curiosity, the Izbek survivor assumed the forms of both the mythical creature on the cave wall and one of the two hominid species inhabiting the valley.

Little did they realize that these Neanderthals would eventually succumb to the rising dominance of Homo sapiens and fade into the annals of history. Understanding the need to form alliances with the dominant species for survival, they briefly took to the skies, gracefully navigating the land when liberated from prying eyes. Feasting upon untamed herds of wild cattle grazing in the fertile valley and indulging in bountiful tuna schools swimming wildly in the Bay of Biscay, they nourished themselves while maintaining a majestic disguise.

Nurturing and guiding the early hunter-gatherers, they bestowed upon them the knowledge of cultivation and animal husbandry, embracing a life of abundance and ease.

Within the pristine valley and majestic mountains lay fertile grasslands, blessed with abundant water and a wealth of untapped treasures waiting to be discovered. Unveiling the secrets of extracting coal and zinc, they enlightened their people on the intricacies of mining, smelting, and metallurgy. As a magnificent dragon, they stood as a protector of their cherished community, revered, and worshipped as a deity by their devoted followers.

Nestled within the protective embrace of the natural fortress of the mountains, the Celtic civilization thrived in what is now modern-day Asturias. This thriving community flourished under the watchful care of the Culebre dragon.

The passage of time found them patiently awaiting rescue in the sanctuary of their cave. At times, they felt the presence of other Izbek, also yearning for rescue. They secretly hoped it was their beloved. Yet, none dared to venture into their realm. Centuries passed and as human minds embraced new enlightenment, pagan beliefs and mythical deities were abandoned. Seduced by the allure of Christianity, their people turned away from the dragon, leaving the Culebre feeling isolated and solely seeking comfort in their human guise. Yet despite their captivating nature, their non-binary existence prevented true acceptance.

As Spain succumbed to the Moors, the lands of Asturias faced imminent peril. In the profound battle of Covadonga, the Asturians repelled the Islamic forces and claimed their independence. Though the Culebre played a vital role, using their mythical amulet to fight, their people credited the symbolic intercession and triumph to the benevolence of a divine statue of the Virgin Mary known as 'Our Lady of Covadonga.'

Recognizing the shifting beliefs of their people, the Culebre chose to leave the land they had called home for millennia, embarking on a journey to reunite with their fellow castaway loved one and seek news of impending rescue. However, as days turned into weeks, weeks into years and years into centuries, they became a nomadic wanderer. Hindered by their homogeneous appearance, assimilation into any community proved a constant struggle, leaving the Culebre in perpetual motion.

Transforming into their majestic dragon self often led to fear, compelling them to continue their travels. Perceived as an evil spirit, a harbinger of destruction in the Middle East and thought to be untrustworthy and viewed as a trickster in Asia Minor and India, their journey pressed on. Finally in the Far East, they found adoration as a symbol of benevolent unity, a bearer of good fortune and a guardian of treasures.

However, even here, their precious purple amethyst became a coveted prize for evil hunters, forcing them once again to flee those enchanted lands where adulation had momentarily made them feel as much at home as in Asturias.

After years of relentless searching, they found peace upon their return to Europe, embraced by the comforting landscape of Wales, a nation proudly associated with the emblem of the red dragon. Nestled under the watchful gaze of Mount Snowdon, they discovered serenity amidst the green valleys, lush forests, and murmuring brooks—a land steeped in the legends of Merlin and King Arthur. Now known as Cinaed Drake, they thrived in this other Celtic realm as an artisan, renowned for their ethereal sculptures depicting the nation's revered emblem—the dragon. Crafted from bronze and carved from blue granite, these masterpieces adorned art galleries around the world.

Seeking solace within their mountain dwelling, which served as both residence and workshop, fiery smoke billowed from their metal forges. Enveloped in a state of secluded bliss, they concealed themselves, their true form hidden from the prying eyes of the world. It is only when the Culebre weaves a cloak of mist and ethereal fog around the mountain that they venture into the skies, soaring undetected and reveling in the liberating embrace of anonymity.

CHAPTER 6

THE WORSHIPPERS

As the Izbek descended to Earth, beholding homo sapiens with curious eyes, they envisioned humans as conduits for their own survival. These ancient beings catalyzed a transformative evolution, gifting humanity with knowledge that birthed magnificent civilizations and scientific wonders. Through subtle nudges towards enlightenment, the Izbek ignited the fires of human progress, inspiring breathtaking feats of art, science, and literature. Leading mankind to dream of traversing the stars.

Across centuries, the enigmatic ancients stood as silent sentinels, guiding human destiny towards the future.

Cloaked amidst the populace, they shaped evolution since their arrival on Earth, orchestrating the course of human history with a deft hand. However, as human advancement surged in recent centuries, unease gripped the Izbek. The rapid growth of sentient technologies posed a challenge.

They would now struggle to temper humanity's progression.

Fissures appeared within the Izbek ranks. Some advocated for limiting human enlightenment while others embraced mankind's evolution.

Amidst these complexities, a consensus arose that the hidden crystals and their immense power posed a dangerous prospect for all involved. Ambitions, avarice, and hubris within humanity could threaten the Izbek and their salvation. With a delicate balance teetering on the edge, the intertwined fates of both humans and the Izbek played out in a fragile dance of historical interplay. As mortals delved deeper into technological innovation, oblivious to the watchful overseers in the shadows, the stage was set for a pivotal moment where intervention could decide the course of evolution.

CHAPTER 7

TRUE CALLING

B ob Sirent, a man with unruly silver hair, a quirky goatee, and mischievous twinkling eyes, swung open the creaky basement door, allowing a rush of cool fresh air to dispel the musty atmosphere that clung to his old house perched atop the steep cliffs of Dana Point.

Overlooking the expansive Pacific Ocean, he marveled at the panoramic view that never failed to amaze him. A knowing smile lit up his face as he realized that his lifelong quest to prove the existence of immortal shapeshifters had finally been confirmed. Bob believed these enigmatic beings descended upon Earth following the last ice age, adeptly disguised as humans while taking on various animal forms, playing essential roles in guiding primitive cultures toward enlightenment and civilization.

To aid his research, Bob transformed his basement into a scientific study that housed ancient scrolls and cryptic texts that lent credibility to his theories. Among his remarkable possessions was an abandoned Russian satellite orbiting in space. With a mischievous glint in his eyes, he ingeniously linked this satellite to his own creation - a dosimeter designed to measure elemental radiation from space. Bob was convinced this radiation would have left an indelible mark on the ancient alien shapeshifters, thus proving their existence.

Imagine his astonishment when his niece and her friends revealed themselves as descendants of the very shapeshifters, he had fervently looked for all his life.

Incredibly, they had the extraordinary ability to transform themselves. Together, they formed a formidable crew known as the "Quad Squad." They transformed his basement sanctuary into a hidden lair pulsating with innovative technology and a central control center for their daring escapades.

On their maiden mission to Lake Mead, Bob's archaic Russian satellite revealed the breathtaking encounter between the Squad, an alien rescue vessel, and the mysterious Izbek. Bob's spirit soared with immeasurable pride, realizing his research had propelled him to this pivotal moment. No longer a solitary scientist in his basement, he had become an integral part of something extraordinary.

Inspired by the Squad's profound connection to the shapeshifters, Bob devoted himself wholeheartedly to their noble cause of protecting the world from malevolence and safeguarding the delicate balance of the environment.

As Bob gazed across the infinite expanse of the Pacific, a sense of newfound purpose coursed through his entire being. Once dismissed by many as a kooky scientist on an elusive quest, he had retreated into his shell, afraid of ridicule. Now, as a mentor to the Squad, he finally realized that his unconventional life had found its true calling.

CHAPTER 8

THE CROCODILE'S RESURGENCE

S obek, the crocodile god, miraculously survived the massive turbines of the Hoover Dam following his fierce battle with Sarah Sirent. Any ordinary person pulled down by the torrent of water into the whirlpool of spinning blades would have been killed. Despite deep lacerations covering his body and the acrid-metallic tang of blood wafting downstream, Sobek emerged alive from the Colorado River. He found himself on a rugged bank beneath the sheltering overhang of Black Canyon. Hidden from sight, the rushing waters muffled his exhausted breaths.

Fate intervened as Sobek had ingested nanites from the Izbek sphere just before his encounter with the dolphin.

These nanites with their incredible regenerative and healing abilities, swiftly began to restore Sobek's crocodilian form. A faint, otherworldly glow enveloped Sobek's body as the nanites worked their magic, casting an ethereal light into the dark canyon.

Fully recovered, Sobek slipped back into the river, determined to reclaim the lost power of the crystals. The cool water against his scales sent shivers of anticipation down his spine. Through his amulet, Sobek sensed that the Izbek rescue ship had disappeared with the crucial information about the crystal's whereabouts. Despite his rage and anger, Sobek knew he had to regroup. Vendettas against the meddlesome dolphin and the other children would have to wait.

Mourning his fallen comrades and in need of a plan, Sobek resolved to reconnect with his trusted lieutenant and friend, Ulf Cadman, the Wepwawet wolf.

Sobek recalled a detail from his time at the dam laboratory that could lead them to a cache of crystals in a conspicuously famous location.

With Ulf Cadman by his side, Sobek would journey to the Highlands of Scotland in search of the hidden cryogenic crystals. He was ever more determined to restore his power and dominance over the world.

CHAPTER 9

NEIGHBORHOOD WATCH

S ituated below rolling hills and just a stone's throw away from the Pacific Coast, the typically peaceful town of San Juan Capistrano had become a place of fear and uncertainty. Several children had gone missing and whispers of a deranged predator on the prowl had spread through the community like wildfire. The entire population was on edge.

At their headquarters in Bob's basement, the Squad watched the disturbing newsfeeds with growing anxiety.

Miles, Ichiro, Jose, and Sarah knew it was time to help and use their formidable abilities as shapeshifters. They could not stand idly by while vulnerable children were under threat, particularly in their own backyard. They had promised the Izbek that they would use their powers to protect the innocent and had also vowed to watch over their families and community.

Desperately trying to position it over the troubled town, Bob tinkered with his surveillance satellite to see anything unusual. However, he would not be able to do so for days.

Therefore, with a sense of urgency, Jose transformed into a majestic eagle and soared above the neighborhood, scouting for any signs of danger.

From high in the sky, Jose's keen eyes scanned the landscape below. He circled over the elementary school, the farm, the busy road, and the sports park. Searching for anomalous activity, he would alert the rest of the Squad if he saw anyone suspicious.

Meanwhile, Miles morphed into a magnificent black panther.

His ebony fur glistened in the fading sunlight as he stealthily prowled through the dense undergrowth alongside the school towards the sports fields. Every sinewed muscle exuded a primal sense of grace, blending seamlessly with the shrubs and bushes.

Ichiro, boasting pale skin and vibrant rust-colored hair, shifted into a majestic fox. As he navigated through the foliage close to the fence, his senses sharpened, attuned to the slightest shifts in the breeze and the faintest rustles in the grass. His lithe form moved with an uncanny nimbleness, honed by his close connection to the natural world.

Although they were an unlikely pair, Miles and Ichiro shared an unbreakable bond forged on their first meeting in middle school.

Their friendship had flourished as classmates, strengthened by their shared understanding of their extraordinary abilities. Like fully drawn crossbows, they were prepared to battle the forces of malevolence.

As the sun dipped below the horizon, painting the sky with fiery hues, the shapeshifters embraced their transformative powers. They prowled the moonlit night as sentinels. Miles embodied a blend of strength and agility. His heightened senses could detect the faintest cries of fear. A fire of intensity burned within him which could not be extinguished.

Ichiro, his russet fur shimmering under the silver moonlight, boasted the cunning and grace of the fox. Each movement carried an air of predatory elegance.

Suddenly, Jose swooped down from the sky, his wings cracking like a bullwhip. Hovering above, he informed his friends that a menacing figure lurking in the shadows close to the basketball court was dragging a large canvas bag towards a parked van near the road. The gravity of the situation became clear. Undeterred, Miles and Ichiro instructed Jose to call the police.

"Alert them of a kidnapping at the sports park," Miles commanded, rushing to catch up with Ichiro who was already in pursuit of the dark figure.

Hunched over and moving toward a van parked near an opening in the fence, a man struggled to carry a large military-style duffel bag. Dressed entirely in black with a hooded sweatshirt, the suspected kidnapper anxiously scanned the surroundings for any onlookers. Unaware of Miles and Ichiro's presence, he did not notice the approaching danger. With remarkable synchronicity, the panther and the fox leaped forward.

Claws and teeth bared; their movements mirrored the relentless fury of nature itself. They struck with impeccable precision and intent. Incapacitated and defeated, the dark figure lay motionless at their feet. Shapeshifting back into their human forms, Miles and Ichiro retrieved the bag laying on the ground.

Apprehension was clearly displayed on their faces as they hesitated to open it, unsure of what they might find.

Once they gathered the courage to do so, inside they discovered a petrified five-year-old boy. His mouth was cruelly bound with duct tape, tears streaming down his cheeks from eyes widened in terror. His entire body trembled uncontrollably while silent screams of fear were trapped in his constricted throat. Miles and Ichiro did their best to soothe and comfort the frightened child, while Sarah, who had been watching with her uncle from the road rushed to their aid. She quickly removed the boy's restraints.

"It's okay, you're safe now," Sarah offered with a reassuring smile. "Do you know where you live?"

The boy nodded, still whimpering uncontrollably.

After discovering the young boy's address, Sarah took his trembling hand and accompanied by her uncle Bob, led him back home, ensuring his safe return to the loving embrace of his worried parents.

With glances of triumph that spoke volumes without the need for words, Miles and Ichiro looked down at the man sprawled on the concrete, his wicked intentions shattered.

As sirens wailed down Avenida Del Obispo, piercing the tranquility of the night, the shapeshifters receded into the comforting shadows of obscurity.

They left the fate of the defeated perpetrator to the police.

As the law enforcement officers uncovered the truth behind the abomination that had tormented the innocent, they unearthed an unspeakable horror. The man who had been mysteriously presented to them for apprehension was wanted for the kidnapping and disappearance of five young children in Arizona. Luckily, the Squad had intervened, ending his malevolent tally.

San Juan Capistrano could once again rest easy, knowing this evil man was behind bars and the Squad was ever present to protect its citizens.

CHAPTER 10

THE WOLF GOD

Rising boldly from the scorching desert sand, mesas shaped by centuries of wind and weather stood tall and proud. Rocky layers, folded and rolled like ancient scrolls, bore silent witness to the spherical silver craft plummeting from the heavens. It skidded to a dramatic halt, leaving behind a swirling cloud of dust and a ripple in the sand. Wepwawet crawled from the wreckage into the unforgiving heat and blinding sunlight. This barren and arid land stood in stark contrast to his aquatic home on Izbekia, where rivers flowed freely nourishing vast lakes and oceans.

To navigate this unfamiliar territory, Wepwawet's powers of transformation would be tested to their limits.

A few hundred yards from his crash site, Wepwawet spotted a cave in the rust-colored cliffs of a towering mesa.

Instinctively understanding the need for shade, he hurried towards the sanctuary of this rocky shelter. Upon stepping into the cave, he found the ground made of a mosaic of stones. The walls were adorned with captivating images that whispered of a forgotten era. Vibrant portrayals of creatures roaming a once-verdant landscape mirrored a time long past before the endless tides of sand swallowed this region.

Quadrupedal beings frolicked in lush green grasslands, while clear rivers teemed with life. Wepwawet wondered what manner of creature had left behind this primitive art as a testament to their existence.

As the night took hold and the scorching sun relinquished its grip, the temperature dropped, casting an icy chill. With the magic of his amulet, Wepwawet coaxed warmth from the cave walls, creating a flickering amber glow.

As dusk gave way to an ethereal silver moon, stirrings of life appeared from hidden places. Centipedes, scorpions, and spiders scurried about in search of food, while furry creatures pensively looked around, frightened by haunting howls echoing through the cave. Golden wolves, like spectral dancers, weaved in and out of the moonlight, captivating Wepwawet's gaze. Clutching his amulet tightly, he transformed into a wolf, mirroring their essence and forging an intimate bond with the night.

Understanding the gravity of his situation, Wepwawet knew he had to look for a less harsh corner of this unforgiving planet. Grasping his amulet, he realized that many of his fellow castaways had found havens more suited for survival.

Though the journey to reach them would be arduous, he knew that reuniting with his former shipmates was imperative, if he hoped to find even a semblance of comfort while awaiting rescue. Moving under the cover of night, in the form of a wolf, he pressed onward to a fertile valley where a majestic river carved its path towards the ocean.

Here, many of his companions had already made considerable progress, securing places where they could thrive. They had assumed the forms of bipedal creatures resembling their own, yet lacking the intricate intellect and capabilities the Izbek possessed. They had also donned the guises of various beasts. Some called the river their home, others soared through the skies and a few slithered on the ground while hunting their prey.

In their superior wisdom, these extraordinary beings could choose to emulate any living creature, granting them an undeniable advantage over the inhabitants of this newfound world. Their supremacy assured, their domination unquestionable.

During their voyage from their home world aboard the Izbek ship, Wepwawet had little interaction with Sobek. However, upon arriving on Earth, an innate connection formed between the two castaways.

Sobek took on the form of a mighty crocodile, reigning supreme over the rivers, while Wepwawet assumed the role of a wolf and ruled over the night.

As time unfolded, an unbreakable alliance began to take shape. Along the banks of the Nile, they forged a magnificent civilization. Mortals worshipped them as gods, bestowing reverence upon them for a fleeting moment.

United by an unwavering bond, they traversed through the annals of history together, inseparable in their pursuit to assert dominance over the planet.

Harnessing the power of humans to further their agendas, they also bestowed upon them intellectual and technological advancements that propelled humanity towards enlightenment.

Their mutual apathy towards the repercussions of manipulating human society only served to fortify the partnership between them.

Yet, the alliance recently met a grave challenge. Bold shapeshifters, the descendants of other stranded Izbek souls, came close to shattering the bond between Wepwawet and Sobek in a deadly confrontation at the Hoover Dam.

Against all odds, Sobek emerged defeated but alive.

Now, they stood poised to reclaim their rightful position as rulers and shapers of the world's destiny. Their journey once again set them on a collision course with the Quad Squad.

This impending encounter, conjuring echoes of the past, would decide the fate of this verdant and enigmatic blue-green planet.

CHAPTER 11

DESTINY UNFOLDS

Following their heart-pounding and perilous exploits at the Hoover Dam, Uncle Bob's basement hideout appeared less captivating to the team. Yet, they had transformed it into an ultramodern communication center.

The once-disordered collection of ancient books and scrolls that filled Bob's basement had been catalogued and organized. Now, wooden shelves lined all four walls, brimming with books of diverse sizes—some with weathered leather bindings reminiscent of autumn hues, while others took the form of modern paperbacks. Despite the improved tidiness, the lingering scent of ancient parchment permeated the air. At the center stood a new metal table adorned with an array of electronic devices. Three solitary electric bulbs cast a soft golden glow across the room, their cords gently swaying in an unseen breeze, creating dancing shadows that added a mystical aura to the space.

The room hummed softly with the electronic buzz emanating from multiple laptops displaying global news feeds. With the aid of mystical amulets gifted by the grateful Izbek survivors, Uncle Bob's ancient computer tower and screen had transformed into a sophisticated control hub. He oversaw a captured Russian surveillance satellite and a functioning supercomputer that scanned for shapeshifting activity in news reports.

"Hey Miles!" Sarah's fingers danced across the keyboard.

"Have you found anything interesting in the news feeds?"

Looking up from his screen, Miles shook his head. "Not yet!

But The Izbek warned us that not everyone could be rescued, so if we are to locate them, we will have to keep looking."

"True." A hint of frustration crept into Sarah's voice.

"We have to live up to their trust. They've put their faith in us, and we cannot let them down."

Seated nearby, Ichiro adjusted the settings on the satellite control panel and remarked with a smile, "we've certainly come a long way from solving math problems in middle school."

Jose, peering over Ichiro's shoulder at the screen, nodded in agreement. "Absolutely. It's amazing to think we've become some sort of superheroes."

Their conversation stopped when Uncle Bob arrived in the basement, carrying a tray of snacks.

"Working hard?" he grinned.

Sarah looked up from her laptop and smiled. "Doing our best," she said. "We cannot afford to miss even the smallest sign. We owe it to the remaining stranded Izbek to find them and let them know that rescue is on the way."

Setting the tray down, Uncle Bob chuckled as he surveyed the room. "You've done an incredible job, and I am proud of all of you. Even if my electricity bill is soaring!"

"You're the best." Sarah hugged her uncle, offering a tender kiss on his cheek that echoed the sentiments of the group.

The Quad Squad had been entrusted with a monumental responsibility by the departing Izbek rescue ship. They keenly felt the weight of this duty, determined to help any stranded Izbek—those who had missed the rescue call due to their depleted amulets' inability to receive the message.

Furthermore, they pledged to protect the planet from exploitation by unscrupulous castaways and shield it from human greed and ambition. Juggling their roles as world saviors with their academic endeavors proved to be a challenging balancing act.

The Quad Squad had transitioned from middle school to Dana Hills High School, proudly embracing the Dolphins as their symbol. They found it amusing that Sarah would fit perfectly as the mascot without requiring a costume.

Their approaching first year student trip promised to guide them through the enchanting landscapes of the British Isles and the bustling city of London. David, Miles' uncle, and Sarah's uncle Bob had volunteered as chaperones, eager to join the adventure. The team was thrilled, knowing that the United Kingdom was steeped in the legends of King Arthur, Merlin, and Excalibur. They were confident that they would not only encounter fellow shapeshifters but also possibly stumble upon Izbek castaways.

Little did they realize; the trip would be fraught with danger.

Once more, they would be called upon to defend the Earth and the course of human evolution, challenging their bravery and resolve in ways they could never have imagined.

CHAPTER 12

MEDICAL MIRACLES

The Garrett Corporation's remarkable advancements in medicine, helped by Jordan's discovery of extraterrestrial technology at the Hoover Dam laboratory, proved to be groundbreaking. In secret, she obtained a microscope slide holding living liquid metal, hoping that this revolutionary solution of microscopic machines would revitalize her family's struggling business in London. With the newfound ability to replicate and synthesize this nanotechnology, her company could now regenerate limbs, repair organs, and potentially cure cancer.

These microscopic marvels held the promise of extending longevity to those with the means to afford them. However, one tragic limitation loomed — the nanites were unable to repair the brain, forever preventing true immortality.

As the head of the Corporation, Jordan Garrett had fulfilled her family's mission to help amputees and instill hope in the hopeless.

She had never contemplated using the technology on herself until the day her aging reflection in the mirror prompted a change of heart. The visible signs of mortality spurred an ethical dilemma within her — was the pursuit of eternal life morally just? Was it mere chance that the Izbek sphere arrived on Earth millennia ago, leading her to unlock its secrets? Was it fate that these secrets granted her the power to reshape humanity forever? These questions consumed her every waking moment.

Weeks turned into months, and Jordan remained plagued by these existential questions until fate intervened. The physical pain on her left side, initially dismissed as a mere discomfort, revealed a grim truth. On Consulting her family physician, Jordan received a devastating diagnosis — pancreatic cancer, a merciless sentence.

Despite her company offering a swift solution through revolutionary technology, Jordan sought a different path.

Remembering her uncle's advice—that when an old car begins to falter, it is time for a trade-in before more issues arise—Jordan considered a radical solution.

The Garrett Corporation had delved into growing human embryos in artificial wombs, watching their development stages closely. Wealthy mothers celebrated the birth of their offspring without the pain of childbirth, a privilege reserved for a select few. Yet, this achievement alone was not enough. With the ability to manipulate individual growth rates, it became possible to have a child delivered as a toddler or older. This process captivated Jordan's curiosity.

The power to condense two decades of development into half a year enticed her, offering a chance to defy destiny as death loomed near.

With immense wealth at her disposal, garnered through her company's groundbreaking research, Jordan envisioned a bold plan — a clone of herself aged 25, having a body as youthful as her spirit. With skilled surgeons and nanites facilitating the intricate neural connections, she aimed to transfer her brain and consciousness to this new vessel.

Soon, she would regain her youth, liberated from the clutches of time, and become immortal.

Empowered by this transformation, she planned to expand her corporation's influence. She would single handily revolutionize global healthcare and safeguard humanity's well-being.

In moments of reflection, tears mingling with her smile, Jordan remembered her family's sacrifices in aiding the afflicted.

Contemplating the implications of her endeavor, a wave of hope and purpose engulfed her. With newfound control over human biology, she saw a future where overpopulation constraints could be overcome, ushering in harmonious coexistence between humanity and nature. An existence free from perpetual strife.

As she envisioned a world devoid of war, famine and suffering, Jordan believed in meticulous planning as the cornerstone of success. Limited resources would need to be managed prudently to avert strain and scarcity, ensuring society's stability.

An enlightened few, like herself, would regulate births and deaths, guiding humanity towards a balanced existence bereft of historical hardships. In her idealistic world individuals would pursue happiness unhindered, freed from the burdens that had plagued generations.

As a sense of certainty enveloped her, the envisioned utopia seemed flawlessly perfect. As if her destiny was intricately woven into the cosmic fabric and had been written in the stars.

CHAPTER 13

TRAGEDY IN BALI

Esteemed archaeologists, David, and Evelyne Cawtheray left on a captivating expedition to Bali Indonesia, drawn by the allure of the ancient Pura Besakih temple. This awe-inspiring structure, perched majestically on the terraced slopes of Mount Agung, loomed high above sea level. It was shrouded in a sacred-mystical aura and whispers of a long-forgotten god. The grandeur of the stratovolcano reaching ten thousand feet into the heavens, cast a spell of both magic and reverence over the land. The Cawtherays fixated on temple complexes mirroring other megalithic wonders across the globe. Here in Bali, their curiosity veered towards a hidden cavern deep within the volcano's embrace. Here, time's relentless march had weathered a forsaken structure, leaving behind a tapestry of crumbling walls hidden behind lush vegetation that had reclaimed the ancient mysteries waiting to be unraveled.

Within the dimly lit recesses of the cave, intricate carvings and faded pictographs whispered tales of yore. Achintya, the divine figure, descended from the celestial realm cloaked in human form encircled by a halo of fire. The Cawtherays, driven by the allure of discovery, ardently believed this forgotten sanctuary marked the pivotal beginning of Indonesia's religious tapestry; the birthplace from which all later civilizations blossomed.

Achintya, a god beyond conception, symbolized the diverse fabric of existence. He was a divine teacher that imparted knowledge coursing through the veins of all living beings.

Still standing defiantly in the deepest heart of the cavernous complex were twin stone thrones, sculpted in the delicate likeness of lotus blossoms. Elegant swans adorned the spaces beside them, straining against the weight of the symbolic flowers they held aloft. One throne gleamed with Achintya's radiant visage amidst ethereal flames and celestial beams. while the other cradled his wife Sarawati who wore a sacred amulet believed to house the very essence of her husband's divine omnipotence and power.

For weeks, the sporadic grumbling of the discontented volcano disturbed the tranquility of the island, releasing plumes of smoke into the sky. Local whispers dismissed these signs as mere murmurs among the gods.

Only the elders recounted the harrowing tales of the devastating 1963 eruption. Pyroclastic flows, searing through villages and cold lahars born of torrential rains, claimed countless lives in their tragic dance of destruction.

Undeterred by the mountain's hidden fury, David and Evelyne pressed forward, their hearts set on unraveling the mysteries of the ancient cave sanctuary. Their scholarly spirits danced with anticipation, oblivious to the approaching storm.

As they delved deeper into the temple labyrinth, the mountain stirred in discontent. The ground shook violently and a low rumbling sound rattled the stone structures. The heavens opened and released torrents of rain upon the land, transforming the once serene landscape into a battleground of chaos and raging waters. Evelyne, her mind consumed by the pursuit of knowledge, found herself trapped within the temple's ancient walls as the rain cascaded with relentless fervor. Panic seized her heart as the entrance collapsed, sealing her fate within the confining grip of a narrow corridor.

"David! Help me I'm trapped!" Her voice laced with desperation, resonated against the storm's raging din, lost in the maelstrom surrounding her. Fear gripped David's heart, each beat echoing the impending tragedy. Fueled by adrenaline, he clawed at the unyielding rocks, determined to free his beloved wife from the clutches of fate.

"Hold on Evelyne. I will get you out!" Water seeped relentlessly through the cracks in the narrow corridor's damp rocks, transforming the once sacred space into a perilous trap.

"Oh God! Oh God! Oh God," Evelyne's anguished cries echoed against the suffocating walls, merging with the fierce fury of the torrential rain lashing the island of Bali.

David's heart pounded as he fought against time and the unyielding deluge, his hands slipping on the slick stones with each desperate attempt to halt the rising tide.

"No! No! No!" David screamed, panic tightening its grip as the water crept higher, threatening to engulf everything in its path. Evelyne's urgent screams grew fainter as she struggled against the relentless surge, her strength waning with each passing moment. Only feet apart, the agonizing proximity intensified the torment of their separation.

"Evelyne!" David's voice cracked with anguish, blending with the storm's thunderous roar. Tears mingled with the rain on his cheeks as he collapsed to the unforgiving ground, consumed by defeat and anguish.

The storm raged on, mourning the tragedy within the ancient temple's walls. Once a sanctuary of wonder, now a testament to fate's cruelty, the cave became a somber tomb, a haunting reminder of love tragically lost. As the monsoon storm continued its wrathful symphony, David was a shattered man in the labyrinth of his own sorrow. His grief weighed heavily upon him; a burden too heavy to bear beneath the rain-soaked Indonesian sky.

After Evelyne's premature death, David was consumed by overwhelming grief, a mere ghost of his former self.

Retreating from social life, he sought solace in his work, which gradually drained his vitality as despair took hold.

Nightmares tormented his sleep, haunted by his wife's dying screams.

Years later, another tragedy struck as David's sister vanished, leaving him the sole hope for his young nephew Miles. Determined to spare Miles from foster care, David opened his heart, welcoming him into his home and breathing new life and purpose into his existence. Raising a child left little room for self-pity.

Now employed at the renowned Archaeology Department at the University of Irvine, David and Miles left behind the somber skies and sad memories of the past. With newfound hope, they aspired to forge a brighter future under California's radiant sunshine.

CHAPTER 14

THE SCOURGE OF WARRIORS

I n the deep recesses of Celtic mythology, a shadow of darkness and mystery looms large with the arrival of The Morrigan, an ancient malevolent goddess who descended to Earth in a silver orb from distant stars.

Accompanied by ominous ravens and eerie giant eels, her presence heralds the horrors of war, enigmatic prophecies, and the manipulation of fate. The Morrigan, a figure of chilling allure and foreboding power, inspires fear in the hearts of mortals, hovering over battlefields in the form of a raven, a harbinger of doom.

Capable of shifting forms at will from a colossal eel to an enchanting seductress, The Morrigan weaves a web of enchantment. She lures unsuspecting souls with her charm while concealing sinister intentions beneath her beguiling guise. Fueled by the power of the moon and adorned with the Triskelion cartouche symbolizing perpetual change, she embodies the cyclical nature of existence. Her very essence mirrored the waxing and waning of the moon.

With each phase and season, The Morrigan metamorphoses into a captivating yet menacing force, forever intertwined with the intricate tapestry of Celtic legend. Her piercing gaze invokes both dread and fascination in those who meet her, a reminder of the ever-shifting currents of life and destiny.

If you venture through a low stile and brave the single strand of electrified cattle fence, traversing 200 yards of lush grazing land, you will come upon the Clochafarmore standing stone. Towering impressively at 10 feet high and 4 feet wide, this ancient sentinel marks the hallowed ground of a long-forgotten battlefield. It is here that Ireland's greatest hero, Cuchulainn, met his untimely demise.

Cuchulainn, a noble warrior, boasted unparalleled skill in martial arts and weaponry. The very essence of his name, which means "battle hound," reflected the ferocity he displayed on the field of combat. However, his life was forever shadowed by a curse inflicted upon him by the Morrigan, the shape-shifting enchantress. In her guise as a captivating maiden, she had approached Cuchulainn, yearning for his affection. Yet, when he scorned her advances and accused her of thievery, her wrath knew no bounds. Vowing to end his life, the enraged Morrigan conspired to hinder him in battle.

During the infamous Cattle Raid of Cooley, Cuchulainn defended the province of Ulster against the forces of Queen Maeve of Connaught. Queen Maeve, driven by a desperate desire to own a renowned brown bull, saw its immense value to rival the powerful white animal owned by her husband. Diplomatic negotiations with offers of gold in exchange for the prized animal proved fruitless. Determined to grasp what she coveted; Queen Maeve unleashed her army upon the unsuspecting Ulster men at a time when their ranks were decimated by disease, a pestilence attributed to the Morrigan's curse by superstitious soldiers.

Yet, in the face of overwhelming odds, Cuchulainn valiantly stood alone and single-handedly repelled the enemy for three grueling days. Though his bravery remained intact, the brown bull he fought to protect was lost to Maeve's clutches.

Nevertheless, the Queen could not shake her gnawing fear of

Ulster's growing power. She turned to the dark arts and the aid of the Morrigan. Her chosen champion, Calatan, a skilled sorcerer, marched forth. Fueled by ambition, he looked to advance his notoriety by slaying Cuchulainn.

However, his aspirations were shattered when he fell before the mighty warrior's blade. Calatan left behind a pregnant wife who raised their sextuplets – three boys and three girls – nurturing them in the ancient arts of druidry. Fueled by a thirst for retribution, they held a solemn vow to avenge their father's death once they reached adulthood.

As time passed, news reached Cuchulainn of the triplet sons' battle cry and their burning hatred towards him.

Unfazed by the imminent conflict, he mustered his resolve to face his foes. He subdued his faithful steed, Lia Macha and harnessed her to the chariot, though she displayed clear reluctance. Tears flowed from the eyes of the magnificent horse, a sight never seen before, as she cautiously stepped into the traces. Accompanied by his charioteer, the hero readied himself for the impending journey.

As Cuchulainn pressed onward towards the battlefield, his heart pounded with determination. He crossed a babbling brook, where an old woman, her voice laden with an eerie premonition, declared that she was washing the very armor of Cuchulainn. She foretold of his impending death. Despite the shiver that ran down his spine, he chose to disregard her ominous words and urged himself forward.

Yet fate seemed to smirk at his defiance and soon he found himself at the mercy of another old hag. This time, she was roasting dogs over a crackling fire. With a mischievous glimmer in her eyes, she invited him to partake in the feast.

Cuchulainn, bound by his sacred vow to abstain from consuming hound meat, hesitated. Yet, his unwavering honor as a warrior compelled him to accept the hospitality.

As he partook in the forbidden meal, a strange sensation washed over him. It was as if his very strength and essence began to ebb away. Unbeknownst to him, this beguiling woman was none other than the Morrigan herself, exacting a punishment upon him for his rejection of her advances.

She had tainted the food, sapping him of his vitality and vigor.

Undeterred by the waning of his might, he pressed forward, looking to fulfill his duty as the defender of Ulster. Yet the three sons of Calatan soon blocked his path. Alongside them stood Lugaid, the son of Cu Roi another man Cuchulainn had previously slain. These cunning foes had learned of a prophecy claiming that the first three spears cast by Cuchulainn in battle would bring mortal wounds to three kings. Desiring to wield these spears themselves and seize control of their destinies, his enemies sought to wrest them from his grasp.

With steadfast resolve, Cuchulainn retorted, "Never let it be said that I am not a generous person," and he hurled the sphere towards his foe. The first son, struck by the deadly weapon, fell to the ground mortally wounded. Lugaid, fueled by vengeance, retrieved the spear, and retaliated, slaying Cuchulainn's skilled charioteer known as the king among all charioteers.

Undeterred, the second son stepped forward, demanding a spear like his fallen sibling. Without hesitation, Cuchulainn answered with a resilient smile, his aim unwavering. The spear flew, and found its mark in the second son, who too met his tragic fate. Lugaid, gripped by a thirst for triumph, returned the spear as his own weapon of retribution, ending the life of Lia Macha the noble steed who stood as a king among horses.

Unyielding in the face of adversity, the third son mocked Cuchulainn's lineage. He insulted his mother and demanded a spear. Cuchulainn grasped the sphere, determined to uphold his family name. The weapon flew once more and ended the life of the mocking son.

Lugaid distracted the mighty warrior, seeing an opportunity for ultimate victory. He retrieved the sphere and unleashed it upon Cuchulainn himself, delivering a fatal blow to the noble fighter's stomach.

With his lifeblood ebbing away, Cuchulainn summoned his last ounce of strength and dragged his weakened body towards a nearby standing stone. Gripping it tightly, he bound himself to the granite block. He refused to die while lying on the ground. For three agonizing days, he stood bound to the rock, a testament to his unyielding spirit. None of his enemies had the courage to approach to see if he was dead.

In those decisive moments, the Morrigan, the harbinger of his doom, transformed into a raven and perched upon his shoulder. As time passed Cuchulainn remained motionless.

Driven by a desire for a final trophy, Lugaid attempted to pry Cuchulainn sword from his grasp. In the struggle that ensued, the sword slipped free. The grim hand of fate intervened when the blade fell and severed Lugaid's arm. An ironic twist that sealed his own fate.

Cuchulainn, an unparalleled king among warriors, succumbed to the malevolent influence of the Morrigan. He joined the ranks of fallen heroes, forever etched in the annals of history.

CHAPTER 15

A CLASH OF CULTURES

I n the vast and rugged lands of Greenland, the stage was set for a clash between two great civilizations. The Vikings, under the leadership of Thorfinn Karlsefni, had arrived to colonize this newly discovered territory, their longboats slicing through the frigid waters with unwavering determination. Opposing them were the Inuit, the native inhabitants of Greenland, who watched the newcomers with a mixture of curiosity and caution, their sharp eyes reflecting the piercing winds that swept across the icy tundra.

Greenland's raw beauty captivated Thorfinn and his men. Its jagged cliffs and fjords presented a striking and familiar backdrop to their ambitions.

The air crackled with energy and tension. Clad in furs and armed with swords as sharp as the northern stars, the Vikings felt whirlwinds of excitement coursing through their veins.

In contrast, the Inuit moved with grace across the frozen landscape, their sleek kayaks gliding over the icy waters as their black eyes scanned the horizon for any signs of intrusion. They shared a deep connection to the land, each footstep echoing centuries of ancestral wisdom. Though their weapons appeared crude compared to the Vikings' arsenal, the Inuit honed each harpoon and knife to deadly precision, a testament to their survival in the unforgiving wilderness.

As the Vikings began to set up settlements in Greenland, unfurling their distinct red-and-white banners, the Inuit watched with a blend of awe and apprehension. While they understood the Norsemen's thirst for exploration and expansion, a protectiveness stirred within the Inuit. They called this land their home.

Communication between the two groups became a challenge, a dance of gestures and fleeting expressions. The Norsemen tried to trade their trinkets and tools for the Inuit's treasures. A vibrant red cloth exchanged for a precious pelt. With laughter traded for curiosity. Despite their divergent languages flowing like rivers in different directions, a fragile understanding began to take shape, akin to a delicate ice bridge spanning a frozen fjord.

Yet fate had other plans in store. A Norse bull, startled by its unfamiliar surroundings, broke free from its enclosure and galloped through the Inuit village. Chaos ensued. The people interpreted the bull's flight as an act of aggression, sparking fear and confusion that spread like embers on a cold winter's night, fueling the fire of conflict.

With an anguished cry and a clash of steel, the Inuit launched an attack on the Viking settlers. The air vibrated with the clash of worlds and the cries of men. What was once unity in curiosity now transformed into a dance of survival, with weapons gleaming like ice shards in the pale sunlight.

The Vikings, their swords unsheathed and shields clashing with fury, stood unwavering, determination etched upon their battle-scarred faces. However, the Inuit fought with a primal grace, their harpoons finding their mark with precision and their knives swiftly slicing through the air.

Every movement testified to their profound bond with the land, guided by whispers of their ancestors.

Suddenly, amidst the chaos and carnage, a figure appeared from the heart of the blizzard. Enveloped by the deafening crackling of purple lightning bolts that electrified the icy air, Nanuk, the polar bear shapeshifter goddess appeared. Her glistening white fur stark against the snow-laden landscape, she advanced with an aura of power. Her ice-blue eyes held a wisdom that transcended mortal struggles.

Silence enveloped the land as all attention turned towards Nanuk. Towering over them, her thick white fur glistened like moonlit snow, while her crystalline eyes exuded wisdom and power.

Nanuk's voice echoed through the frozen valleys, compelling both the Vikings led by Thorfinn Karlsefni and the Inuit to lower their weapons and embrace peace.

Entranced by Nanuk's presence, a sense of awe and unity washed over them. It transcended cultural boundaries, nurturing a shared humanity.

With ethereal elegance, Nanuk spoke of the land's potential and the need for harmony and collaboration, weaving vivid tales of bountiful rivers, seas, and unexplored horizons. She conjured visions of the Northern Lights' beauty and the whispers of ancient spirits, guiding them towards mutual comprehension and cooperation.

In that pivotal moment, the Vikings and Inuit exchanged knowing glances, acknowledging the intertwined nature of their fates. Thorfinn extended a hand of friendship, met with resolute acceptance by the Inuit leaders. This marked the dawn of a new alliance founded on mutual regard and collaboration.

United by a common purpose, the Vikings and Inuit blended their distinct knowledge and skills. Through shared teachings and joint endeavors, they gleaned wisdom from each other, nurturing a bond that transcended past strife and enmities.

As the seasons unfolded, guided by Nanuk's vigilant

gaze, Greenland blossomed into a testament to unity and understanding's might. The once-antagonistic civilizations prospered in harmony, crafting a legacy of resilience, empathy, and cooperation that inspired future generations.

The people of Greenland reflected on their shared past with gratitude, venerating Nanuk as the catalyst for harmony. A monumental totem depicting Nanuk clutching a magical amulet arose as a symbol of their collective odyssey and enduring accord. A reminder of peace triumphing over discord in their realm.

With their ancestors' spirits as witnesses, the Vikings and Inuit embraced the everlasting ties forged amidst the clash of civilizations, bequeathing a legacy of unity and coexistence in Greenland's rugged terrains.

CHAPTER 16

THE DISCONCERTING TEXT

Professor David Cawtheray, Miles' uncle, returned to the University of California Irvine, and its archaeological department. His mind was in turmoil from a mix of shock and bewilderment after the unsettling encounter at the Hoover Dam. There, he grappled with alien technology and witnessed ruthless mercenaries killing a colleague. It affected him deeply. It stirred a contradictory tempest within him.

There was no doubt in his mind about the extraterrestrial origin of the sphere.

"Why else," he deduced, "would there be such keen interest shown by various entities and the strict secrecy imposed on him by the United States government?"

The peculiar discoveries made by the research team hinted at an extraordinary influence from beings not of this world on human evolution. This knowledge upended the very foundations of history and his own academic understanding.

When he shared the entire escapade with Sarah's uncle Bob, it did little to alleviate his disquiet.

"Could the progression of human civilization have been accelerated by the infusion of alien DNA and technology?" he pondered.

If Bob's conjecture about a race of alien beings arriving on Earth just after the last Ice Age proved correct, many of history's enigmas could potentially be solved.

The mysteries of the Great Pyramids, Stonehenge, and the Nazca lines in Peru could be unraveled. Humanity could shed light on their unexplained ingenuity in ancient times and around the globe.

David had extensively studied creation myths to gain insights into their cultural significance and impact on early societies. Despite the profound implications of his newfound knowledge, he worried his peers would ridicule him as a crazed madman should he dare to share his hypotheses.

As a result, David fell back into a daily routine, concealing the storm of thoughts brewing beneath his calm exterior.

As David concentrated on his professorial duties at the university, the memories of Nevada began to fade away.

However, change was on the horizon.

Several months later, David received a cryptic message from Jordan Garrett, his late wife's closest friend, and former colleague from the Hoover Dam project. The message shattered the veneer of normalcy in David's life, imbuing urgency and mystery while hinting at a revelation of profound importance that demanded his immediate attention.

Jordan's plea transported David back into the state of uncertainty that he thought he had left behind.

After they left the Dam and pledged a vow of secrecy about their encounter with alien technology, Jordan had returned to England to focus on her ailing medical company. David felt a pang of sadness at her departure, sensing a connection between them.

Upon receiving the text, David promptly decided to reach out to Jordan, eager to rekindle their bond.

"What's the matter? How are you holding up?" David inquired, genuine concern palpable in his voice.

Jordan hesitated momentarily before responding, "I'm... I'm okay."

She paused; her voice quivered as she continued. "Well not really. I desperately need your advice, but I am too anxious to discuss it over the phone. Can you please come to London?"

David noticed the urgency in Jordan's voice.

"Why the haste? Is everything all right?" he probed.

"Yes, but I can't explain here. I really need your help."

Jordan's voice wavered.

David contemplated whether her distress was linked to their encounter with the government officials who had interrogated all the scientists at the Hoover Dam. They had issued dire threats if they divulged details about the millennia-old spacecraft.

Luckily, fate intervened. Miles and his peers were set to embark on a field trip to the British Isles the following week.

Although David initially hesitated to volunteer as a chaperone, not wanting to ask for another extended sabbatical away from work, Jordan's plea prompted a change of heart. "Jordan of course I can come to London next week. I will arrange everything," he replied.

"Oh my God! Thank you so so much!" Jordan felt relieved, her gratitude resonating through the phone.

As the conversation ended, David could not help but wonder why Jordan sounded so terrified.

CHAPTER 17

CRUEL DECEPTION

A long the rugged shores of Scotland, where the sea and sky embrace in a timeless dance, exists a mesmerizing being known as the Selkie. Enchanting and alluring, she unveils her captivating beauty with each graceful shift from seal to human form. She is more at home in the depths of the ocean than on land, finding comfort in the ebb and flow of the tides.

To beguile humankind the Selkie takes on a physical appearance that is a testament to her otherworldly nature.

Her flawlessly smooth skin seems to radiate with a seductive luminescence, as if touched by the very moonlight that guides her nocturnal wanderings. However, it is her eyes that captivate all who meet her, beholding a depth of emotion that few mortals could understand. Within her soulful obsidian gaze, hopes and dreams intertwine, drawing those who meet her into a realm of enchantment.

The Selkie's mane of long silvery hair cascades down her back, shimmering like the metallic undertones of a stormy sea. Flowing like liquid mercury, it whispers untold secrets and forgotten stories, a subtle reminder of the duality that lies within her very essence.

In her benevolence, the Selkie offers guidance and protection to those who treat her with kindness, becoming a beacon of hope amidst the raging tempests and treacherous waters. Yet, the Selkie possesses a duality. Beneath her ethereal beauty lies a dangerous and vengeful spirit, ready to unleash an unforgiving fury upon those who dare to cross her.

To meet her is to witness the very essence of nature personified. She is a reminder of the eternal battle between the crashing waves and the unyielding shores, each striving to achieve the delicate balance needed for existence within the two realms the Selkie inhabits.

Appearing from the heavens like a celestial bolt, the pod collided with the snow-dusted peak, careening down the mountain slope with thrilling recklessness. It continued its wild journey along the icy-blue glacier below, before finally coming to rest. The pod tumbled from the frozen cliff face, plunging into the crashing surf below and slowly sinking under the waves.

In such a predicament, most beings would have succumbed to panic and terror. Yet, the Izbek castaway was intimately acquainted with the ever-enveloping ocean. On her home world, the majestic seas offered moments of respite where the Izbek communed with the collective consciousness and embraced tranquility.

Though she harbored little hope of contacting her fellow castaways, she clasped her amulet tightly, closed her eyes in telepathic concentration and sent forth her prayers.

However, the silver sphere resting amidst the swaying kelp beds received no reply. Despite the lack of response, her presence attracted iridescent fish and deep-black-eyed figures with smooth, grey-dappled skin gracefully navigating the waters nearby.

Intrigued by her inquisitive spectators, the castaway ventured into the icy embrace of the water. The freezing temperatures felt like a million sharp needles piercing her fragile frame, starkly contrasting the cozy waters of her home planet. Assuming the form of her aquatic observers, she at once felt warmth, comfort, and peace. These creatures, with their gentle spirit, embodied simplicity, and joy. Unbeknownst to her, this form would sustain her for millennia as she awaited rescue. This chosen avatar would fuel the ebb and flow of her relationship with the land dwellers, swinging between symbiotic harmony and outright conflict.

After several daring forays to the surface and dry land, the survivor found the terrain above the waves less inviting. A dominant bipedal species roamed the land, hunting, and consuming other creatures with relentless voracity. Realizing their advanced nature, she adopted their form to survive in the green landscapes of forests and grasslands. While her amulet shielded her identity, the potency of the planet's single moon meant she could not risk its exposure. Thus, when traversing the land, she cautiously concealed the mystical amulet near the water's edge before engaging with humanity.

In human circles, she relied on her heightened mental acuity and beguiling charm to sway and seduce the primitive beings, securing what she needed for her continued safety and survival.

Logan Currie, a local fisherman, lived in the quaint village of Mikladalur, near a secluded cove. Towering cliffs surrounded this enchanting place. Weathered caves dotted their rocky walls, while majestic sand dunes guarded the beach. Within the village, Logan grew up hearing tales of a mythical seal creature. Folklore told of her appearances from the depths of the ocean under the radiant glow of the harvest moon, transforming into a mesmerizing beauty that captured the hearts of all who beheld her.

Logan, a practical man, brushed off these stories as mere superstitions concocted by bored bachelors in the local tavern, yearning for affection. However, one fateful autumn night changed everything. As the giant moon ascended from the horizon, illuminating the shoreline, and casting its radiant glow upon the cove, he watched in disbelief.

From his position above the beach, Logan spotted a purple star sparkling in the water. Shining brightly, it glided past his anchored rowboat towards the shore. Intrigued yet cautious, he concealed himself among the tall marram grasses that grew atop the dunes and peered through their waving blades.

Before his amazed eyes, a graceful grey seal emerged from the sea, wearing a mysterious purple jewel. As if touched by magic, the seal transformed into a bewitching woman.

Her mercurial hair cascaded down her back, framing an alabaster complexion. Her eyes, as dark as ink with an irresistible allure reminiscent of black diamonds, completed her captivating visage.

Logan, consumed by desire and longing, found himself utterly captivated by the beauty before him. He vowed, then and there, to woo her in the hope of making her his wife.

But he knew that if she returned to the sea, such a union would never be possible.

From his hiding spot, Logan watched as the Selkie carefully concealed her precious amulet beneath a glistening rock near a time-worn cavern at the base of the cliff.

As the enchanting creature made her way towards the village, Logan's curiosity mingled with trepidation. He seized the moment and stealthily crept towards the cave, retrieving the jewel from its secret nook.

With the amulet safely stowed aboard his boat, Logan rowed across the bay, heart pounding, until he reached his humble abode. There, he locked away the treasured stone within a sturdy wooden chest, securing it with a key that he carefully fastened around his neck. Returning swiftly to the cove, he anxiously awaited the Selkie's return and her frantic search for the crystal that held the power to transport her back to the gentle embrace of the sea.

Feigning innocence and disguising his own crime, Logan approached the Selkie, posing as a Good Samaritan eager to help her. Unable to return to the waters and with no other alternative, she reluctantly accepted the fisherman's perceived kindness and went with him to his home.

Days turned into weeks and weeks into years, as the fisherman and his enigmatic companion tirelessly returned to the cavern in search of her lost necklace. When their efforts proved fruitless, the Selkie eventually resigned herself to the life of a fisherman's wife and bore him several children.

Though she appeared content, her heart held a deep longing to return to her watery homeland, beckoned by the serenading songs of the relentless waves crashing against the rocks close to their home. Cruelly, the instrument to reunite her with her underwater community lay hidden within the very walls she now inhabited.

As the years went by, hope faded and resignation took hold, until one night, her husband's drunken revelry at the local tavern led to a moment of forgetfulness.

As Logan went off to fish, he inadvertently left the key to the hidden chest behind to be discovered by the youngest daughter of the Selkie who brimmed with curiosity. As her nimble fingers delicately turned the key, a sense of anticipation swelled within her. The creaking sound of the chest opening echoed in the air.

Within its confines lay an assortment of treasures, but it was a single item that stole the young girl's attention. Nestled amongst iridescent seashells and velvet pouches holding silver coins, was an enchanting amulet that seemed to radiate with an otherworldly glow. Her eyes widened with wonder as she held it up to the light, its intricate details sparkling like the dancing sun on the ocean's surface.

Breathless with excitement, the young girl carefully placed the amulet around her neck. Instantly she felt an inexplicable connection to its ancient power. A surge of warmth coursed through her veins as if the amulet recognized her as its rightful guardian. Filled with joy, she hurried to her mother, her eyes sparkled like stardust, eager to share her discovery.

Caressing her daughter tenderly the Selkie removed the necklace and cradled it to her chest, tears cascading down her cheeks. Filled with sadness and betrayed by such deceit, the Selkie retreated to her watery sanctuary beneath the waves. While she assured her children that she would return occasionally to visit and frolic with them in the tide pools, her heart burned with a thirst for revenge. She vented her anger not solely at Logan but at all of humanity daring to defile and exploit her beloved ocean.

Upon Logan's return home, his rage grew as he discovered the empty chest and the Selkie's absence. With the anger of a man scorned, he callously sent his children to live with his sister in the village. From that day forward, fishing and hunting seals consumed his existence, reveling in the gruesome trade of their meat and pelts.

Meanwhile, the Selkie's outrage swelled, vowing to avenge her lost kin and the years she had wasted with a deceitful husband. Her wrath knew no bounds as she declared her vengeance against Logan and anyone endangering the safety of sea creatures. With unyielding anger, she pledged that her fury would persist until mountains of human bodies stretched down to the darkest depths of the ocean's trench.

As centuries drifted by, the Selkie watched from her watery realm with sorrowful eyes. She saw humans slaughtering sea creatures for food, hunting whales for their valuable oils to fuel their growing cities and polluting her once tranquil domain. Massive factory ships ravaged the ocean's treasures and left behind desolate, lifeless wastelands.

Realizing she could no longer remain idle, the Selkie reluctantly returned to land, mingling with humans.

Disappointed to discover that some of her castaway comrades

had aided in humanity's technological advancements, she wished her amulet were as vibrant as it once had been. With its diminished power, it became impossible to reason with them and increasingly challenging for her to return to the sea. Yet, when the moon shined in all its brilliance, she found a way to do so.

It appeared that the Izbek, whom she had hoped would rectify the crimes of their rogue members and save her, would never come back. Undaunted, as the centuries advanced into modern times, the Selkie, now known as Isla Selch, vowed to combat humanity's destruction and strive to safeguard the delicate balance of the ocean's ecosystem.

Embracing her new identity, Isla immersed herself in influential positions within environmental activist circles.

She joined esteemed organizations such as Greenpeace, Oceana, and Friends of the Earth International.

Recognizing the critical situation of species on the brink of extinction and the pressing need to protect and restore the world's oceans, Isla became a fervent advocate. Despite understanding the delicate balance these organizations had to maintain, navigating between the needs of vulnerable coastal communities and the constant requirement for funding, Isla pursued a more assertive and proactive approach, free from bureaucratic interference.

Joining The Global Protection Initiative, an organization committed to taking decisive action, she found herself immersed in their mission. Coincidentally, their annual meeting was to take place at the enchanting Aldourie Castle hotel in Scotland, nestled alongside the mystical shores of Loch Ness.

CHAPTER 18

ENVIRONMENTAL SOLDIERS

I n the 21st century, a formidable entity known as The Global Protection Initiative appeared. Its influence spanned the corners of the globe, uniting a diverse group of affluent individuals. The elites perceived themselves as the rightful inheritors of a global order.

However, as their dominion and privileges waned, concerns began to surface within their ranks. They viewed the working class as constant consumers of essential resources such as water, clean air, and food that the elites believed should primarily be reserved for themselves.

Driven by self-interest, one of their goals was to manipulate the so-called civilized world into withholding aid from underdeveloped nations that grappled with disease, famine, and overpopulation.

Stemming from the fervor of the man-made global warming movement and ecological green crusades, their beliefs morphed into a more militant ideology. These conservation warriors held humanity accountable for the planet's desecration, attributing it to widespread fossil fuel use and the emission of harmful substances into the atmosphere.

They contended that these activities intensified the greenhouse effect, leading to a perilous rise in global temperatures.

GPI stood out as the most radical faction within the climate activism movement, viewing natural disasters like droughts, earthquakes, floods, and diseases as purifying agents of Mother Nature. They believed these events served as effective tools for population control and restoring harmony.

During the devastating drought in sub-Saharan Africa, which claimed many lives, they perceived it not as a tragedy but as nature's stern hand working to restore equilibrium.

In the past, charitable organizations and governments played a significant role in providing aid to those in critical need. However, this emerging order believed such endeavors were ineffective and worsened the prevailing issues. They argued that the masses were unwilling to adopt the drastic measures necessary and were oblivious to the level of force needed to achieve the desired equilibrium.

Unbeknownst to billions worldwide, the GPI engaged in a perilous global game, guided by those secluded in their ivory towers. Exploiting ignorance, the wealthy and privileged unleashed pathogens into water supplies, manipulated weather for destructive purposes and devised intricate plans to induce devastating floods.

The most recent triumph of their malevolent agenda remained concealed behind the veil of the global pandemic.

Through compliant news services and widespread internet propaganda, they skillfully obscured their involvement in orchestrating the outbreak, ensuring it appeared natural and untraceable. Under the guise of pursuing "Global Balance," the world's elite deluded themselves into believing that their actions were indispensable and just.

They vehemently repudiated the idea that their relentless pursuit aimed to safeguard Earth's dwindling resources was solely for their benefit. Instead, they reveled in their extended lifespans courtesy of exclusive medical advancements accessible only to the privileged few.

While ordinary individuals went about their daily routines, they were tragically oblivious to this ominous scheme, mere pawns in a darkly cloaked game. Within this intricate power web, Isla Selch, the shapeshifting Selkie, aligned herself with this faction not out of affection for its leaders but driven by a resolute determination to halt humanity's invasive expansion into her undersea realm. The construction of wind farms that claimed the lives of her fellow sea creatures needed to stop. The pollution and floating debris jeopardizing wildlife and contaminating the waters had to cease.

The acid rain corroding coral reefs could not be allowed to persist. Moreover, the undersea mining operations causing widespread destruction in their wake had to be outlawed.

Isla believed that restraining world population growth could pave the way for a brighter future. Anticipating the annual meeting of GPI at a hotel along the shores of Loch Ness, Isla eagerly looked forward to gaining insights into how GPI could bolster her individual crusade.

CHAPTER 19

THE BLACKSMITH KILLER

Slinking out from the dark shadows, the Bouda prowls as a specter of the night, a chilling embodiment of the were-hyena intimately linked to the essence of the nocturnal realm. Its eyes, a malevolent amber hue, pierce through the darkness, to peer into the depths of one's soul with unsettling intensity. A palpable stench of death and rotting flesh clings to its mottled fur, an olfactory testament to its gruesome existence. The putrid dance of decay that follows in its wake attracts not only the vultures circling above but also the attention of those brave enough to watch the macabre spectacle.

In its gnarled grip, the Bouda clutches a wooden scepter adorned with a mesmerizing purple stone glistening within a six-sided star setting. This ethereal glow emanates ancient wisdom and foreboding enchantment. It grants the Bouda the ability to seamlessly transform from human to beast.

Hailing from the distant north in the land of Canaan, the Bouda journeyed across vast expanses of arid deserts and perilous mountain ranges to reach its present domain.

Murmurs born on the winds accompanied its arrival. They recounted stories of unmatched metallurgical mastery and blacksmithing expertise, whispered to be known only to the gods.

With sly agility, the Bouda navigates the shadows, moving through concealed alleyways and secret pathways with an almost supernatural grace. The night air echoes with its eerie joyless laughter, an unholy chorus signaling the impending approach of death. One of the most fearsome aspects of the Bouda's existence lies in its role as the devourer of the dead. It is the collector of souls, preventing them from passing into the afterlife. It revels in this grotesque duty, relishing the power it holds over the delicate balance of life and death.

The Bouda, master of the macabre, embodies the darkness lurking within the depths of our fears, serving as a haunting reminder that not everyone's soul is granted passage beyond the veil.

In a time long forgotten, the Bouda was not a creature of shadows and dread. Once, it was a shapeshifting god known to the people as Hendursaga, revered as a divine night watchman and torchbearer, bringing an ethereal purple light to the darkest corners of existence. He was a guardian against the malevolence that lurked in the depths of the world. However, Hendursaga's insatiable ambition led him to challenge the might of Enki, the patron god of the revered temple of Eridu in the heart of the Fertile Crescent.

Such audacity did not go unnoticed by Enki, who considered Hendursaga's actions a direct affront to his divine authority.

In a fit of righteous anger, Enki cast Hendursaga out from the sacred lands of Mesopotamia, condemning the god to a life of exile and solitude. Ashamed and resentful, Hendursaga sulked despairingly southward, far from the lands he once called home.

But Hendursaga was no ordinary deity. His ancient knowledge of smelting and metallurgical techniques became his disguise, allowing him to seamlessly blend in with the impoverished local people. No one suspected that the humble blacksmith, with hands calloused from years of labor, was the banished god in disguise. To further aid his concealment, Hendursaga carried an ordinary wooden scepter adorned with a glistening amethyst crystal. This jewel had mysterious powers, enabling Hendursaga to transform at will, independent of the moon's phases. With this newfound ability, the creature now known as the Bouda could roam the vast savannah, causing chaos under the veil of darkness.

As time marched on, in the heart of Somalia where the golden sun casts its fierce rays upon the African landscape, the terror of the Bouda became entwined with the intricate tapestry of Somali folklore, a chilling tale that sends shivers down the spines of the native people. It tells the story of a fearsome were-hyena that has plagued the region for centuries.

Amidst the arid savannah, nestled within a humble village, there stood a rustic forge belonging to an inconspicuous blacksmith. During the day, he would diligently toil with molten metals, crafting intricate works of art and practical tools that served the needs of the community. The village revered him for his unparalleled craftsmanship, unaware that his heart harbored the tainted essence of evil itself.

But as the sun sank beneath the horizon, an enchantment would seize the peaceful visage of the blacksmith, transforming him into a twisted beast. No longer did he have the essence of a man; instead, he became the embodiment of terror itself. His body elongated, limbs contorted, and once-kind eyes turned blood-red. The Bouda was unleashed.

Under the pale moonlight, night after night, the creature prowled the untamed African wilderness, preying upon unsuspecting victims. It traversed the land with an otherworldly agility, its monstrous paws leaving deep imprints in the dust as it hunted. The stench of death wafted in its wake, mingling with the earthy musk of the savannah.

Mothers in nearby villages, as twilight ominously approached, abruptly halted their daily chores, and gathered their children close, their eyes filled with a mixture of fear and love. The air itself held its breath, carrying the weight of hushed whispers, telling tales of the Bouda's insatiable hunger, the grotesque crunch of snapping bones and the spine-chilling echoes of silenced screams that permeated the night.

The African landscape itself became an integral part of this harrowing legend. The winds whispered secrets to the moonlit trees and the moon, an ever-watchful eye, cast eerie shadows that danced like specters across the plain.

The sounds of nocturnal creatures, usually comforting, now echoed with a sense of urgency - a cacophony of chatter conveying imminent danger.

Even the animals themselves cowered when the Bouda prowled. The proud lion, king of the savannah, would flee at the slightest hint of its presence. Fear gnawed at the hearts of all living beings, for it was not only the Bouda's victims who fell under its chilling grasp; it was the dread that engulfed an entire region.

Generations passed and the legend of the Bouda persisted, woven into the fabric of the Somali people's consciousness.

They learned to respect the darkness and fear the encroaching nightfall, for they knew that within the veils of gloom the were-hyena appeared, ready to tear souls from living flesh.

And so, to this day, as the sun begins its final descent, mothers still clutch their children tightly, whispering words of protection against the lurking terror. The Bouda may remain nothing more than a whisper, but the weight of the legend remains heavy upon the hearts of the native people, reminding them of the eternal dread that goes with the coming of night.

Bouda dedicated countless years to seclusion, honing his blacksmithing skills with unwavering determination. Despite his continuous efforts to uplift the local community from poverty and improve their lives, they stayed distant and fearful of him. He eventually realized that his current situation held no prospect of acquiring gold or power. So, Bouda made the decision to venture north along the Nile River, in the hopes of reuniting with his former people.

However, to his profound disappointment, he discovered that they had long vanished, their powers fading into obscurity. Undeterred by this setback, Bouda resolved to settle down. He decided to use his vast knowledge and ability to resurrect a semblance of his former glory.

Millennia had passed since Bouda, a castaway from the Izbek race named Hendursaga, crash-landed near the vibrant Tigris River where he found himself amidst a primitive and malleable people who willingly worshipped him as a god. The disagreement between Hendursaga and Enki, though ages ago, still lingered within his heart.

However, he harbored little concern for the fate of his fellow crewmates and their whereabouts.

In modern times, known as Bouda Napach, he stood as the prominent figure behind Qori Ismaris Steel Company, Egypt's leading manufacturer of steel rods and rebar. The company's symbol, a sturdy scepter adorned with a vibrant purple crystal held in a six-sided steel star setting, paid homage to the heritage of its founder.

Renowned for producing some of the finest metal products in the world, Qori Ismaris Steel played an instrumental role in the construction of national landmarks, such as the Museum of Egyptian Civilization, the Rod El Farag Axis Bridge, and the newly built Cairo monorail. Every time Bouda caught sight of these unmistakable pyramidal structures and the bustling transportation hub, memories of his distant home planet, Izbekia flooded his thoughts. The manufacturing foundries and steel mills he owned in Alexandria and Port Said were strategically located close to bustling trade routes, facilitating the distribution of his products worldwide.

Maintaining a close partnership with the Sobek Corporation, Bouda relied on their fossil fuels to ignite his furnaces and the necessary raw materials from their mining company.

Martin Krugler and Ulf Cadman, his fellow survivors and Izbek castaways, had helped his arduous passage long ago through ancient Egypt to the lands of Somalia. Nowadays, their reunion did not mirror that of fellow gods but unfolded as business partners. However, it had been quite some time since Bouda had laid eyes upon Martin and Ulf, as they had made their home in New York City.

Thus, it came as an astonishing surprise when his personal assistant, Amina, informed him one radiant morning at his ultramodern high-rise office in New Cairo that Ulf Cadman, the Wepwawet Wolf God of ancient Egypt, had arrived for a meeting.

As Ulf entered the room, wearing a sleek dark-grey suit that complemented his wolf-like features, Bouda stepped forward to greet him.

"My old friend! It seems like an eternity," Bouda exclaimed.

"Ulf I can't believe it is really you! What brings you here?"

"Well. once Sobek and I realized that you created this steel empire, we wanted to connect with you to partner in something important."

"Please sit down," Bouda offered. He was eager to hear what Ulf had in mind.

CHAPTER 20

GLOBAL PANDEMIC

C enturies ago, Wepwawet the Wolf and Sobek the Crocodile, ruled over the lands of Egypt, revered, and worshipped as divine gods. Their advanced Izbek technology allowed them to create vast cities, to live in comfort and to garner great power and wealth. However, as time passed, their once-glorious amulets lost their luster, and the source of their extraordinary strength faded away.

Finding themselves adrift, the Izbek desired fervently to replenish their power. Together, they began their quest to find the miraculous triOsmium crystals. These ancient artifacts, seeded on Earth by the mothership before its departure, held the promise of restoring their position as gods. In search on them, they journeyed through countless landscapes and civilizations.

With each passing year, Wepwawet and Sobek sought new ways to influence the development of humanity, to keep a semblance of control and power. In 1347, destiny led the shapeshifters to the crossroads between Asia and Europe, to the Crimean Peninsula on the shores of the Black Sea. They shadowed the Muslim Golden Horde, a powerful Tartar army, posing as trusted advisors.

Utilizing their subtle influence, they directed the Horde to conquer the wealthiest countries and cities; to plunder the unimaginable riches they needed to reclaim their dominance. Among these conquests, the port of Caffa stood before them like a shimmering gem. This city held a treasure trove of gold, jewelry, and exotic goods from both Europe and the Far East.

As the two former gods plotted to enrich themselves, fate intervened with a cruel twist. The Mongols had besieged the city for months, yet their efforts were abruptly halted by a deadly disease. This pestilence, borne by rats carrying fleas, had traveled along the Silk Road and infiltrated their camp.

Faced with the devastating onslaught of the plague, the Tartar soldiers lost hope and interest in the battle. However, within Wepwawet and Sobek, a twisted determination grew.

Immune to the disease's grasp, they watched the chaos unfold from their tents and devised a malevolent plan.

Utilizing their command positions, the shapeshifters ordered the troops to catapult the infected dead bodies over the city walls. Unbeknownst to the inhabitants of Caffa, doom was descending upon them. With each diseased body that crashed into the city, death and misery infiltrated its very heart.

Rotting corpses tainted the air, poisoning the water supply and engulfing Caffa in a putrid miasma. The Christian citizens, trapped and unable to flee, tried to dispose of the dead, desperately casting their bodies into the sea. Panic gripped their souls as they believed that even a mere glance from an infected individual would spread the poison.

Days stretched into weeks, and the silent grip of the plague tightened its hold. Caffa, once a vibrant and bustling city, now lay as a desolate ghost town, its dwindling population falling prey to the ghastly disease known as the Black Death. The shapeshifters watched with twisted satisfaction as their scheme unfolded, crippling European societies, and casting a dark shadow over the entire world.

The contagion, carried on the winds and through human

interaction, spared no city, no settlement, no soul. Men, women, and children alike, regardless of status perished, their bodies overcome by agonizing pain, their senses overwhelmed by the stench of death. Boils, black and putrid, erupted on their once-vibrant flesh, oozing the very essence of the plague itself. The medical friars and doctors were helpless, their knowledge and remedies futile before this malevolent pandemic.

Initially believed to have originated in Central Asia and China, the Black Death embarked on a relentless path, hastened by the shapeshifters' treachery at the Battle of Caffa. Fear became a constant companion, with the specter of imminent demise weighing heavily on the hearts of the people. Societies crumbled, economies collapsed and as the deadly plague extended its reach globally, civilizations fell.

Panic gripped the populace. Once-thriving societies transformed into desolate ghost towns, their streets lined with the decaying bodies of the innocent. Pandemonium reigned and the shapeshifters, Wepwawet and Sobek, reveled in the chaos they had wrought.

Their malevolent plan had achieved its desired effect. With the population drastically reduced, the shapeshifters seized immense fortunes and power, capitalizing on the devastation wrought by the Black Death. Their treachery had not only secured their wealth and influence but also cemented their reign of terror over the shattered remnants of society.

The world plunged into profound darkness. The sudden cessation of human activity, including farming and development, resulted in an unforeseen consequence. With fewer humans exploiting its resources, the Earth experienced a resurgence of life. The absence of humankind enabled the majestic forests to reclaim their territory, spreading like a verdant carpet across once-barren landscapes. As the trees flourished, they served as guardians against the relentless rays of the sun, shielding the Earth from its scorching embrace. The drop in global temperatures was so profound that it triggered a chilling phenomenon known as the "Little Ice Age" that blanketed the world in frost and ice.

Wepwawet and Sobek took pleasure in manipulating human behavior. In their twisted game, they exploited religious teachings and superstitions, shifting the blame for the pestilence and bitter cold to the will of God. Gripped by fear and desperate for a scapegoat, the people of Europe fell prey to their manipulation. Innocent Jews, caught in this grand charade, became the targets of hatred and persecution. Massacres ravaged cities like Cologne, Mainz, and Strasbourg, leading Jewish communities to flee eastward in search of refuge in Poland. Sobek and Wepwawet once again profited from the confiscated wealth.

Together, they laid a solid foundation for their quest for global domination. Wepwawet and Sobek evolved, shifting locations as they adeptly capitalized on opportunities to amass power and influence.

Today, they are known as Ulf Cadman and Martin Krugler.

From their ill-gotten wealth, they have risen to positions of power as owner and senior executive at the Sobek Corporation, a formidable conglomerate in New York City.

Steering the company towards the exploitation of Mother Earth and fossil fuel extraction, their influence spans the globe. Exerting control over the media, Krugler and Cadman shield themselves from public scrutiny. This control over information dissemination is crucial, especially for the corporation's most nefarious operation. Deep within their organization, a division dedicated to studying and manipulating pandemic pathogens— a deadly weapon within their arsenal—poised to be deployed if they chose to impede human progress and halt the evolution of mankind once again.

CHAPTER 21

THE CHANGING TIDES

I n the heart of the Scottish Highlands, where ancient mists cling to the rugged landscape, people whisper a tale from generation to generation. It tells of a mythical shapeshifter, a creature born of tempest and darkness, known as the Boobrie.

Legend tells of how this enigmatic being descended from the heavens, conjured from a mighty storm that raged through the celestial sky before time began. Like a fallen star she plummeted to earth, her landing marked by the crashing waves of a Scottish loch against a towering glacial wall. It was there, amidst the haunting beauty of the wilderness, that she made her home.

From the very beginning, the Boobrie reveled in her transformative powers, manipulating, and guiding the early residents of the land to her whims. She bestowed occasional favors upon them, but in her heart, she was an exploiter, using their trust for her own gains. They were mere pawns in her grand scheme, game pieces to be played as she awaited the opportune moment to ascend once more to the heavens.

In her true form, the Boobrie was a fearsome sight. With wings spanning the width of seventeen majestic eagles, she transformed into a monstrous avian creature akin to a cormorant. Jet-black feathers cloaked her towering frame, while her immense wings beat through the air, casting a shadow that could eclipse the sun. Her short, webbed feet left imprints upon the earth, resembling human hands, a sinister reminder of her presence.

Yet, the eyes were her most unnerving feature. Black as the abyss, they held a piercing stare capable of driving even the bravest souls to the brink of madness. People who dared to gaze, trembled, their minds ensnared by the twisted tendrils of her power.

But the Boobrie's shape was not restricted to the skies alone. Like the ever-changing tides, she could transform herself into a water horse, an equine presence equally at home on land as in the depths of lochs. With each stride, she galloped effortlessly across the mirrored surface of the water, defying the laws of nature and expectation.

An eerie cacophony heralded her arrival, a sound that pierced the stillness of the Scottish landscape. It resonated through the mist-laden air like the bellowing roar of an ancient bull. Those who heard it quivered, for they knew that danger lurked nearby, concealed within the cloak of her monstrous form.

In the summer months, when the sun bore down upon the land, the Boobrie's appearance would change yet again.

Taking the shape of a grotesque insect, she would skulk in the shadows, her predatory nature revealed. Leaving behind a trail of fear and devastation, she would suck the blood from livestock.

But it was in her disguise as a human that the Boobrie's true allure lay. Her jet-black hair cascaded like midnight silk, framing a visage that held an ethereal beauty. Captivating black eyes, accentuated by glimmering highlights that mirrored the stars themselves, held a mysterious charm that lured the unsuspecting closer. In her hands, she held a mystical jewel, a gemstone that mimicked the hues of the moorland heather. Legends whispered that this jewel held the power to command demons from the depths of the lochs, allowing her to conjure thunder, lightning, and torrential rain from the skies.

Farmers who relied on the lochs for sustenance were aware of the lurking presence that awaited them. As they led their animals to drink from the shores, they cast wary glances to the heavens, praying for clear weather. For they knew that if the Boobrie was near, her intentions were far from benevolent. Her spectral form lingered beneath the surface, waiting to claim unsuspecting victims.

Her escape pod had crash-landed in a wondrous landscape, its metallic shell bouncing across the surface and sinking into the sandy shore of the loch. Disoriented, she appeared from the sphere, her senses tingling with the exhilaration of new surroundings. The desolate beauty of the place stretched out before her, both captivating and daunting. The loch itself was a remarkable sight, its dark waters colder and more ominous than those on her home planet. They lay still and deep, mirroring the brooding sky above and the receding glacier at the head of the valley. However, the mere sight of them gave her some comfort, reminding her of the joy she used to have swimming in the vast oceans on Izbekia. On either side of her, the soaring hills rose majestically, adorned with lush vegetation that painted the landscape with vibrant shades of green. Trees, grass, and wildflowers garnished the slopes, their tops a majestic purple hue as the heather bloomed in scattered patches. It was a tapestry of nature's handiwork, a portrait of a land unspoiled and resilient.

Venturing forward, her bare feet sank into the soft sand, leaving imprints that whispered tales of her otherworldly presence. The wind danced through the reed beds, carrying ancient melodies and forgotten legends. The rustling of the tall grass joined forces with the crashing of the waves, creating a haunting symphony that both allured and cautioned her. Approaching the edge of the loch, she extended a hesitant hand to touch the water, drawn towards its enigmatic depths. A shiver of exhilaration ran through her as the icy coldness embraced her fingertips. Her gaze lingered upon the rippling surface, captivated by the reflection of this planet's solitary moon.

Steadying herself against the unknown, she embraced the spirit of exploration, each step an invitation for adventure.

Survival was her priority, adaptation her strength. With each breath, she soaked in the fragrant air, ever ready to unravel the secrets woven into the fabric of this new world.

A glimmer of hope flickered within her as she stumbled upon a peculiar sight. At dawn, she saw a group of bipedal creatures leading animals with four legs to quench their thirst at the loch. They formed a primitive social structure, their rudimentary dwellings standing as reminders of simple ingenuity. Instinctively, she recognized an opportunity. By mimicking these beings, she could forge a more comfortable existence while awaiting rescue.

Her amulet seemed ever brighter as it pulsed with familiarity and she detected the Morrigan, another of her kind not too far away.

A sense of camaraderie washed over her, affirming her choice to take on the forms of the human and avian creatures she encountered. For she knew she was not alone in her plight and together, they would navigate the challenges of this unknown world until rescue arrived.

CHAPTER 22

THE WHITE BEAR GODDESS

As a raging winter storm howled outside, snowflakes pirouetted in the frigid air while a divine presence descended from the heavens. Nanuk, the Polar Bear Shapeshifter Goddess, appeared before the world in a breathtaking spectacle. Her ethereal figure glided to Earth encased in a colossal silver snowball, landing gracefully onto the icy tundra.

Nanuk embodied the essence of winter and the hunt, her purpose intricately woven into the rhythm of nature. With each stride upon the icy ground, the earth quivered in homage to her might and creatures of the Arctic bowed in reverence. She possessed a duality that enchanted those who witnessed her presence. Gentle and compassionate, she safeguarded the delicate equilibrium of life, yet her ferocity and power were renowned. —a force capable of toppling mountains with a swipe of her paw.

In her human guise, Nanuk captivated onlookers. Her snowy white skin exuded an otherworldly radiance, setting off the darkness of her jet-black hair that flowed like an obsidian waterfall. Deep ebony eyes reflected the profound depth of the Arctic night sky, shimmering with ancient wisdom.

Always at her side was a magnificent crystal, imbued with

the enchantment of winter's caress. Nanuk used this precious artifact to conjure snowflakes and icy winds, spreading winter's embrace across her realm. Through her sorcery, she crafted an exquisite ice palace amid the frozen mountains, a magnificent abode from which she ruled over her wintry domain with unparalleled grace.

Nanuk, the polar bear goddess, embodied the delicate balance of beauty and power, nurturing and fierce. Her very presence commanded respect from all who encountered her, instilling a sense of awe and reverence. In her wintry realm she reigned as a majestic guardian, ensuring the harmony and survival of the creatures that inhabited her snowy dominion.

In the remote village of Inuktitut, nestled on the icy shores of the Arctic, lived a young Inuit hunter named Malak. With his harpoon in hand, he ventured onto the frozen polar ice sheet guided by the light of the full moon and the ancient stories shared by his wise grandfather who constantly assured him that he was special.

On this day, as Malak crept closer to his prey, the ice beneath his feet creaked and groaned. Knowing the importance of patience and focus, he ignored the unsettling sounds. But fate had a different plan in store for him. With an earth-shattering crack, the ice split open beneath him, plunging him into the freezing depths of the Arctic Sea.

As his body sank, Malak's consciousness began to fade. The icy coldness embraced him, draining his strength. But just as he was about to succumb to the dark depths, a vision appeared before his eyes. It was a colossal white polar bear, her fur shimmering like freshly fallen snow. This magnificent creature swam gracefully towards Malak, guiding him to the surface with her immense strength. The bear's eyes gleamed with a curious wisdom that seemed beyond the realm of ordinary animals.

Malak awoke on the sandy beach, his body shivering and weak. As he gathered his disoriented thoughts, the warm whispers of his grandfather's stories floated through his mind like a trail of memories. According to ancient legends, those chosen to carry the spirit of the polar bear had incredible strength, wisdom, and a deep connection to Nanuk herself. Returning to the village, Malak sought his grandfather's counsel. With a twinkle in his eyes, the elder confirmed what Malak had suspected. He had indeed been chosen by Nanuk, the polar bear goddess, to carry her spirit within him. Although skeptical at first, all his doubts disappeared when the following full moon cycle he transformed into a majestic snow-colored bear.

Embracing his newfound destiny, Malak trained meticulously, honing his physical and mental strength under his grandfather's tutelage. Being able to transform at will without the aid of the moon, he felt a harmonious bond with the elemental forces of nature, guided not only by the teachings of his ancestors but also by the indomitable spirit of the polar bear.

As time passed, Malak faced a myriad challenges and adversaries, but the spirit of Nanuk burned fiercely within him, guiding him to protect his village from danger. In this frozen landscape and close-knit community, Malak's legend as a special hunter blessed by Nanuk continued to grow. His story— of courage, resilience and the profound bond between man and nature—served as a reminder to all young adults all over the world to listen to the whispers of the wilderness. For within those whispers, there may lay the secrets of their own true potential.

CHAPTER 23

THE MISTRESS OF REVELRY.

In Ancient Egypt, where the realms of gods and humans intertwine, a captivating and enigmatic deity named Hathor descended from the heavens in a fiery chariot.

Associated with music, dance, joy and love, Hathor is honored as the protector of life's most delightful pleasures.

Her essence spans the cosmos, illuminating the very fabric of existence. Crowned with distinctive horns, she holds a mystical bond with the revered temple of Dendera in Upper Egypt, radiating her influence on the lands of Nubia.

As a shapeshifter, Hathor embodies the essence of transformative energy, often taking on the guise of a sacred cow standing for abundance and fertility. Women in labor call upon her divine presence, beseeching for a secure and blessed passage into motherhood. During the transition to the afterlife, she offers comfort, leading departing spirits to their eternal resting place.

Hathor graces the material world. Enchanting melodies, rhythmic dances and enticing elixirs hold a unique allure for her. Devoted followers assemble in her honor, reveling in the sensory pleasures bestowed upon them by their adored goddess.

The air is laden with the fragrance of incense, blending

with heartfelt devotion as offerings to Hathor. Amethyst gemstones, beloved by both the deity and her followers exude a luminous hue. Within the temple, the soothing rattle of sistras interweaves with melodious chants of worship, ensuring eternal bliss and benevolence in Hathor's presence.

Hathor, revered as the mistress of the stars and the sky, holds the key to creation within her majestic horns, symbols of her timeless reign. The grand annual flooding of the Nile, with its waters tinged in passionate red hues reminiscent of wine is a sign of her magnificent influence.

Celebrations dedicated to her essence overflow with vibrant music and ecstatic dance. Hathor intricately weaves the fabric of joy throughout the mortal realm.

She graciously bestows upon her joyous devotees the blessings of music, dance, and spirited revelry, forever celebrating the joys that enrich life's tapestry. Her eternal nature, guiding and benevolent, resounds in joyous symphonies and rhythmic sistra beats, encapsulating the very essence of bliss.

Thousands of years ago, in what is presently Egypt, a thriving and a vibrant landscape existed.

Intef, a respected member of the Badari tribe, diligently carried out his duties in their camp under the watchful gaze of the moon. He meticulously gathered kindling, collecting dried reeds from the water's edge and animal dung from the surrounding trails. Intef's pivotal role centered on tending to the crucial campfires that offered warmth, illumination, and cooking flames for his people.

On this evening, Intef prepared to display his culinary ability by roasting a majestic antelope. With the creature skinned, cleaned, and firmly fastened between two wooden poles, Intef set about creating the ideal cooking fire. Skillfully igniting the kindling, he coaxed gentle glowing embers to life. As the flames waned, he strategically positioned the wooden poles, enabling the antelope to cook gradually and tenderly over the smoldering embers.

The Badari tribe, long acquainted with the challenges of their daily lives, experienced a pivotal moment in their history when Hathor, their guide and protector, descended from the heavens in her blazing chariot.

According to the legend, the transformation of Hathor into a magnificent black bull ensued before she revealed herself as a resplendent ebony woman bedecked in golden attire and jewels. Through her arrival, the Badari's existence underwent a profound shift as she bestowed upon them newfound wisdom and skills.

Under Hathor's tutelage, the Badari tribe no longer needed to forage for plants and fruits or hunt distant herds. She endowed them with the knowledge to cultivate crops and raise their own livestock, thereby transitioning from a nomadic existence to a settled lifestyle.

Hathor's teachings extended to the mastery of woven reed traps, enabling the Badari to harness the plentiful fish swimming in the mighty river. They skillfully tamed tall grasses to mill their kernels into flour, creating bread that appeared almost miraculous in its creation. With her guidance, the Badari adeptly honed their abilities to mold clay into pottery, weave wool sourced from animals into garments and forge copper tools essential for agriculture, hunting, and self-protection.

The goddess Hathor imparted the divine knowledge of fermentation, unlocking the alchemical process that yielded a marvelous intoxicating elixir from grains, evoking sensations of bliss and revelry. This crimson beer mirrored the hue of the river during its annual flood, a time when Hathor would once again take the form of a black bull, immersing herself in its waters to nourish her resplendent coat.

Intef, once burdened by the constant worry of unpredictable weather threatening his fires, found solace in the gift bestowed upon him by Hathor. She presented him with a magical translucent crystal that harnessed the power of the sun. When held toward the radiant star, the crystal would draw the sun's intense radiance, causing the earth to smolder and ignite into flames.

The Badari revered Hathor as a goddess, yet she chose to walk among them as both a priestess and Sabia.

Unceasingly awe-inspiring was the mystical purple jewel she always carried, a conduit of immense power. They had seen Hathor wield this enchanted gem, summoning thunderstorms, and showers, as balls of lightning crackled and electrified the atmosphere.

With a mere wave of her hands, she summoned colossal blocks of granite, marble, and limestone from distant lands.

They defied gravity as they floated upon an unseen river.

Hathor marked her divine presence on Earth with the construction of a magnificent temple.

In the passage of time, the Badari's prosperous community drew the attention of neighboring peoples, who eagerly joined their ranks. Under Hathor's watchful eye as their Bull goddess and the creator of their civilization, Intef and his people flourished. Forever grateful for her heavenly guidance.

CHAPTER 24

CONFLICTING APPROACHES

As the golden rays bathed the city of Dendera in a warm glow, the vibrant colors of the bustling marketplaces burst to life. Merchants haggled animatedly over exotic fabrics, spices, and jewels from distant lands.

Hathor known for her grace and wisdom; commanded attention draped in shimmering turquoise robes. Her obsidian locks, adorned with delicate golden accessories, cascaded down her back like a waterfall of midnight silk.

One morning, as Hathor strolled from the tranquil temple gardens towards the banks of the Nile, she was captivated by the lotus flowers gracefully floating in the calm waters.

The petals of these blossoms painted the scene with a mesmerizing tableau of pink and purple hues. Transformed into a majestic bull, Hathor waded into the water allowing the fragrant floral aroma to embrace the air around her.

In a peaceful moment, Hathor's eyes widened in surprise as she saw Sobek, the fearsome crocodile god appear from the shimmering depths. His presence inspired both awe and disturbance, signaling a troubling revelation about mortal challenges to divine authority.

"Hathor!" Sobek's voice tinged with anger, expressed concern over mortal defiance spreading across Egypt and urged Hathor to crush any rebellion without mercy.

Fear gripped Hathor. She was torn between upholding her gentle nature and the call to assert divine dominance. While she had the courage to protect her way of life, she also recognized the importance of preserving the delicate bond between themselves and humanity.

"Of course," Hathor replied with concealed reluctance. Her voice trembled ever so slightly. "I will do everything in my power to help."

Sobek arose from the water in his human form and nodded in approval. "Very well. Continue to keep your followers in check. If any rebellion arises, inform me and I'll send Wepwawet to crush it."

Slipping back into the river as the mighty crocodile, he disappeared under the floating flowers.

Returning to her ancient temple that rose majestically from the desert sands, Hathor contemplated the unsettling encounter with her fellow castaway. It was disconcerting how he had succumbed to power and greed, contrary to the values of their home world.

She vowed to uphold her heritage and sustain the bond with her worshipers and keep the symbiotic relationship she had forged with humanity.

Integrated within nomadic tribes since her arrival on this planet, Hathor, revered as an ethereal goddess and magnificent black bull, imparted knowledge, and guidance.

Her influence ushered a sedentary culture centered around the Dendera Temple, which stood as a beacon of ancient wisdom.

As Hathor retreated into the inner sanctum, a tranquil coolness enveloped her. Soft light filtered through the high ceiling, casting a glow upon a sublime golden throne positioned at its heart. Enveloped in reflection, she sat down, her heart still thundering from her recent encounter with Sobek.

In that moment, an overwhelming sadness coursed through her veins. She missed the kind heart of Culebre, her soul mate.

Despite the weight of Sobek's words, a flicker of determination ignited in her soul, propelling her to treat humanity with strength and compassion.

She would continue to govern with unwavering resolve, unyielding even in the face of opposition from her former comrades. She would confront them head-on if necessary.

With each passing day, Hathor embraced the necessity of forging a harmonious balance in a world on the brink of conflict. Although she was determined to navigate the challenges with grace and wisdom, in a moment of intense reflection she longed for Culebre.

CHAPTER 25

HARBINGERS OF BAD FORTUNE

For centuries in Ireland, the people revered the Morrigan as a deity, embodying the essence of fortune and fate. However, with the rise of Christianity, she found herself displaced, her once-mighty influence waning under the fervor of Saint Patrick's arrival.

The Morrigan boarded a ship and with a heavy heart she watched as the Emerald realm, her ancestral homeland faded into the distance. She traveled to Scotland, where she sought solace in the land of other Celtic tribes. In the depths of the captivating and mysterious Loch Ness, she found the Boobrie, her kindred spirit. This fellow female survivor, a being of similar grace and beauty, offered her companionship and an alliance that would surely withstand the trials of time. Together, in an eerie and foreboding house overlooking the inky murky waters of Loch Ness, the Morrigan and the Boobrie lived as enigmatic creatures of the night. Cloaked in shadows and concealed from prying eyes, they waited for the day when rescue would come, all the while exploiting without remorse the resources and people nearby. Instead of becoming benevolent overseers, they ruthlessly took whatever they needed to survive.

Adorned with amulets of deep purple pulsating with ethereal energy, the very essence of her power, the Morrigan felt her strength restored with each passing day in this new land. No longer diminished by the rise of Christianity, she stood together with the Boobrie as formidable as when she first graced this ancient world. Her amulet, once thought to be fading, now gleamed with otherworldly brilliance, a testament to her extraordinary power and the jewels beneath the Loch.

Rumors of witchcraft began to spread among the local villagers. Whispers carried on the winds, spun tales of sorcery and malevolence. To the unsuspecting villagers, the Morrigan and the Boobrie were the catalysts of misfortune.

They were blamed for every disaster that befell their land.

When floods swept through the villages, when plagues of crows ravaged the crops and when livestock and people vanished into thin air, it was the dark veiled figures by the loch that the villagers accused. When the brave Highland warriors fell to defeat at the nearby Battle of Culloden Moor, butchered and slaughtered by the English, the crows that picked at the corpses were rumored to have been sent by the Boobrie and her evil companion.

Little did the villagers know, their suspicions grazed the truth. Unbeknownst to them, the Morrigan and the Boobrie possessed the power to shift their forms, delving into depths unknown. Beneath the surface of Loch Ness, one transformed into a colossal eel, her movements a sinister graceful dance of power, while the other became the mythical water horse arising from the depths and galloping across the glitter path on the water's surface, dancing in the moonlight. Each of their existences was a testament to the aura of this wild and rugged country.

Feeding on the abundant fish, otters and farm animals that ventured too close to the water's edge, the Morrigan and the Boobrie reveled in their supernatural connection.

Although lacking proof, the frightened villagers suspected that the monsters they conjured up in their darkest tales were, in fact, these very beings they feared.

Over time, the whispers turned to legends and legends became entwined with the very fabric of the loch and its surrounding lands. The Morrigan and the Boobrie, still lingering in the shadows, continued their vigil, waiting for the rescue that might never come. As long as they dwelled by Loch Ness, its waters would forever remain cloaked in mystery.

CHAPTER 26

BEWILDERING TRANSFORMATIONS

Sarah's uncle Bob, an enigmatic man in his fifties with a pitiful goatee and an ever-increasing head of grey hair, could not help but feel an overwhelming sense of satisfaction. After years of whispered theories and hidden research, the Squad's extraordinary abilities had finally proven his wildest hypotheses to be correct. Ancient alien shapeshifters did in fact exist. However, he could not bask in the glory of his vindication. Sarah and the rest of the Squad had sworn Bob to secrecy. Therefore, he chose to keep his groundbreaking discoveries to himself and instead became their invaluable ally. He too dedicated his life to the mission of safeguarding Earth from sinister forces and helping guide the young heroes when called upon.

By necessity, the Squad transformed Bob's cellar into their secret headquarters. Sitting atop a cliff in Dana Point, Bob's magnificent home offered mesmerizing vistas of the expansive cobalt-blue Pacific Ocean. But the true heart of their Lair lay hidden beneath the living quarters, in the basement where Bob toiled away daily, consumed by his studies of extraterrestrial beings. To the Squad's delight, the entrance, once a simple door, was now down a secret passageway concealed behind an automated sliding panel masquerading as an ordinary bookcase.

Thus, ensuring that the Lair stayed a secret sanctuary. In case of emergencies, Bob now kept a speedy getaway boat waiting at the bottom of the cliff. A serpentine staircase leading onto the cliff face via the other door in the basement led directly to the beach.

The transformed basement was now a technological marvel.

Rows of gleaming laptops hummed with digital life, their screens displaying a constant stream of global anomalies.

Bob's commandeered satellite, orbiting high above, offered an aerial view of the world's unfolding mysteries. And there, amidst the pulsating energy, the Squad discovered more amazing facets about their amulets that gleamed with latent potential.

For a while, since the Squad's amazing meeting with the Izbek, nothing of significance had taken place and tranquility had reigned supreme. Yet as if summoned by fate, a whirlwind of peculiar tales began to filter out from the British Isles. These uncanny reports hinted at something extraordinary brewing in the Scottish Highlands, signaling a convergence of events that would challenge the Squad like never before.

"It has to be shifters," declared Miles. "Witnesses claim to have encountered flying creatures, ghosts and monsters."

He revealed many accounts of strange events from local newspapers, social media, and personal blogs.

"It's likely connected to the crystals," Sarah added, her voice filled with concern.

"If that's the case we've got a problem," Ichiro interjected.

"That's for sure." Jose, quiet until now, chimed in. "But who precisely is after the crystals? Are they friendly or not?"

He shook his head.

"We need to get there," Miles instructed. "We're all signed up for the London field trip. That will be our chance to find out what's going on."

The Squad had volunteered Bob to be their chaperone, and he eagerly accepted the role. The chance to advance his research and finally meet the beings he had been searching for all his life compelled him to say yes.

"Isn't your uncle joining us too?" questioned Sarah, looking at Miles.

"He is." Miles confirmed, then he paused, looking pensive. "I think it's time to let him in on our secret. After the incident at the Hoover Dam, I'm sure he suspects something. After all, we share similar DNA."

"How will you tell him?" Jose inquired. He had no such worries. His grandfather already knew about his particular abilities.

Recalling how they had previously revealed their powers to Bob by demonstrating their abilities, the Squad agreed upon the same strategy for Miles' uncle. They decided to invite him to the secluded cove beyond the headland beneath Bob's cliff-top residence.

As Sarah's uncle and David stood before Miles and his companions, the moment to reveal their avatars arrived.

"What is this all about?" David asked, perplexed by the specific choice of location beneath the cliff.

The Squad collectively smiled and exhaled, closing their eyes to embrace the exhilaration coursing through their veins. A profound sense of liberation, like a waterfall cascaded through their bodies. Each teenager began to undergo a mesmerizing transformation: Ichiro morphed into a wily fox, feeling his bones reshape and his russet and gold fur gleam. Miles embodied a panther, reveling in the ripple and flow of his muscles beneath his reflective black coat.

Jose expanded his arms as feathers burst from his fingertips, transforming him into a majestic hawk. And finally, Sarah, merging with the essence of the sea, transformed into a dolphin, her opalescent skin shimmering under the ocean's surface.

Upon opening their eyes, primal energy surged through every fiber of their beings, forging a connection to the wilderness and freedom itself.

David sat on the beach astonished, visibly trembling at the extraordinary scene unfolding before him. He was flooded with countless questions. "Where does this ability originate? And how long have you known?" David queried breathlessly.

"Have you always been aware of this power. And, how in heavens name do you control it?"

Miles calmed his uncle and helped him up.

Bob, having experienced the same transformation months before, steadied himself and comforted David.

"Take a deep breath David," Bob instructed in a soothing and steady voice. "I understand this is overwhelming."

As the sun began to set, casting a golden hue on the ocean, the Squad gathered around David to explain their origins, the mystery of their amulets and the mission to safeguard Earth.

Each member shared their personal journey, and the challenges faced in embracing their newfound abilities.

David listened attentively. His shock turned to awe and curiosity. With each revelation, his eyes grew wider, and his mind brimmed with boundless possibilities.

"So, all this time, you've been secretly doing good deeds?"

David marveled, filled with admiration.

"We have," Sarah affirmed, determination shining in her eyes. " But with your support, we can make the Squad even stronger."

A newfound sense of purpose swelled within David's heart as he realized the extraordinary nature of the mission. This was another chance to play a significant role in something larger than himself.

"I'm in," he said and pondered the connection between the

events in the British Isles, the Hoover dam incident, and his recent conversation with Jordan Garrett.

As the waves crashed on the shore and the stars appeared in the night sky, they embraced their new destiny as a formidable team prepared to confront the unforeseen challenges ahead. Unbeknownst to them, the journey to the Scottish Highlands would mark a pivotal moment, pushing them to their limits and unraveling secrets beyond their imagination. Fate had intricately woven their path forward. It would test their strength, loyalty, and belief in themselves.

CHAPTER 27

THE SEARCH FOR LOVE LOST

Nestled along the winding banks of the Nile, the ancient and vibrant city of Dendera seemed to breathe with life. Majestic pyramids rose into the sky, casting shadows upon the colorful streets below.

Obelisks, like imposing sentinels stood tall, their hieroglyphics telling stories of the gods.

Hathor, draped in flowing garments of gold and blue, embodied the essence of love, beauty, and fertility. Her presence radiated a warmth that touched the hearts of all who met her. Humble farmers to ambitious pharaohs, revered her as the caring and compassionate goddess.

As the tides of time swept across the land, Hathor's influence transcended the borders of Egypt. After the conquest of Alexander the Great, her celestial persona resonated with the people of Greece and Macedonia. They knew her as Aphrodite, the goddess of beauty and love. And with the rise of the Roman Empire, she assumed the mantle of Venus, the goddess of joy and springtime, spreading her divine aura across the boundaries of that bygone empire.

Yet deep within her heart, Hathor longed for Culebre, her lost companion with whom she had forged an unbreakable bond in the vast oceans of Izbekia and during their journey across the cosmos. Alas, during their descent to Earth, their escape pods, despite being launched in quick succession, had not fallen to Earth with the same velocity. They were separated in the vast unknown.

In her deepest dreams, under the silver luminescence of the moon, Hathor's heart quickened, anticipation coursing through her every fiber of being. It was then that Culebre, her long-lost love, descended from the heavens above. As whispers of nature swirled around them, Hathor's gaze met Culebre's luminous eyes. An electric surge of emotion jolted through her immortal veins, as if time itself had paused. In a tender embrace, their forms melded into one, a testament to the infinite bond they shared. The ancient love between Hathor and Culebre transcended the realm of slumber, unbreakable oaths woven deep within them.

After many centuries of loneliness and with unwavering determination, Hathor embarked on a quest to find her lost mate. She traversed distant lands, seeking any clue that would lead her back to her beloved Culebre. She hitched her journey to the might of the Roman army and traveled as a prophetic oracle, predicting the outcomes of battles, and guiding their conquests.

On her travels in the ancient forests of Gaul, she encountered Aatxe, a fellow shapeshifter. Aatxe had chosen the form of a bull as her avatar, mirroring Hathor's own divine transformation. Together, they reveled in the fertile pastures of ancient France, accompanying the Roman legions as they marched North. However, Aatxe held no knowledge of Culebre's whereabouts.

Undeterred, Hathor pressed on with the Roman legions, crossing the treacherous waters of the British Sea to reach the distant shores of Britannia. York, or Eboracum as it was known, greeted her with its relentless rain and somber skies. The streets glistened with dampness, reflecting the gray granite that pervaded the land. It was vastly different from the sun-drenched banks of the Nile, where she had reveled as the epitome of joy and dance.

As Hathor ventured further north, the landscape transformed before her very eyes. Standing near the ancient structure known as Hadrian's Wall, a formidable barrier that separated the south from the savage wilderness of the north, she felt the biting chill of Cumbria. The wind whipped through the harsh-spiny marram grasses and carried with it sweeping sleet and rain from the desolate moors. Hathor's heart carried an undeniable sense of urgency, for she believed that some of her former crew mates, scattered and lost, lived among the warring and savage Pict tribes north of the wall.

She was reluctant to journey further north. Venturing into this hostile territory meant putting her life in peril. Yet, it was her deep loyalty and love for Culebre and those she had once sailed alongside through the universe that propelled her forward. With determination as her guiding light, Hathor scoured the lands north of Hadrian's Wall, seeking information and forging alliances to aid her in her quest.

Within this treacherous landscape, she crossed paths with a wise and mystic druid.

Clad in black plaid robes and with his face adorned with a striking blue pigment, the Celtic shaman exuded an air of ancient knowledge. He knew of one of the scattered kin Hathor sought. With the druid's guidance, Hathor infiltrated the mysterious lands of Caledonia by assuming the form of a majestic black bull.

The barbarous tribes marveled at this ethereal deity that stood before them, awed by her otherworldly presence. The Pict tribal leaders, struck with both fear and reverence, began to realize that Hathor's intentions were peaceful.

With eloquence and grace, she pleaded to their Celtic heritage, explaining that unlike some of her kin, she was not an adversary but a protector of the Earth and the heavenly realm.

Amidst the mist-laden moors and among ancient castles, Hathor walked with the same grace as she had when surrounded by the swirling desert sands. Through heather-capped hills that overlooked tranquil lochs, whispered tales of battles fought, and victories won resounded in the valley.

The wind, a gentle companion, rustled through her hair, urging her forward.

As Hathor ventured deeper into the highlands, she finally found the Boobrie, one of her former comrades and fellow castaways. Miraculously, her amulet gleamed with increased brilliance, leading her to suspect that a cache of triOsmium was somewhere nearby.

Mist clung to the landscape, a mystical veil designed to conceal age-old secrets and ancient magic.

The Boobrie, living beside a black lake, had forged a purpose among the tribes, where she was both revered and feared. Joy washed over Hathor upon their reunion, and they exchanged tales of their earthly experiences.

However, it became clear that their paths had diverged significantly. Hathor, known as the embodiment of love in ancient Egypt, found herself in stark contrast to the Boobrie.

Her fellow castaway dwelled away from humans who feared her influence on the fates and the capriciousness of climate, fire, and ice.

Despite the renewed power surging into her being from her magnificent purple jewel, Hathor realized the dwindling commonality with this reunion. Hathor left the Boobrie and returned south to the city of Eboracum, where she set down roots and found comfort in its historic embrace.

The years rolled by. Remnants of Roman architecture whispered tales of past grandeur, while the medieval streets carried the weight of countless footsteps. As Hathor made her home amidst these humans, she elegantly portrayed the strength and majesty of a bull, reservedly revealing her true nature only when necessary.

Through the passing ages, Hathor bore witness to the ebb and flow of empires, personally experiencing the magnificence and ultimate decline of the influence of the Romans. She stood on the banks of the river, watching as Viking longboats, adorned with fearsome dragon heads sailed upstream, ushering in a wave of change and chaos.

The winds of transformation blew as Christianity swept across the land from the mainland, leaving imprints of its influence. The towering Minster, a testament to this newfound faith, rivaled the splendor of any structure she and her fellow Izbek had built along the Nile. Yet, even amidst the cathedral's majesty, remnants of her own kind endured. The Masonic workers, with their ancient knowledge imparted by the Izbek, carried the secrets of their craft, symbolized by the Masonic flying eye symbol of Ra. She watched as the valiant William Wallace, the Scottish nationalist, battled for his country's freedom, boldly capturing York in his noble quest to sway the heart of England's king. The War of the Roses unfolded before her eyes; a conflict that shaped the very course of history, its impact reaching far into modern times, deciding the path of kings.

As ages rumbled by, in the depths of her immortal heart, Hathor held tight to the glimmering hope of reuniting with her long-lost partner. Millennia had passed and her magical amulet, once a beacon of connection to her kin, had once again dulled with time. Though she carried the weight of uncertainty, she diligently observed the ever-changing world, awaiting the salvation and rescue that only the return of the Izbek could bring. She clung to the dream that one day, when the Izbek finally returned, they would find all the castaways including her beloved Culebre and reunite her with her soulmate.

CHAPTER 28

THE PLASTIC FUTURE

Martin Krugler, once the formidable Egyptian God Sobek and now the esteemed leader of a rapidly expanding oil conglomerate, had amassed immense wealth by the late 1920s. Amidst the chaos of the Wall Street Crash and the Great Depression, most investors watched their fortunes crumble. Krugler however, a cunning oil tycoon, skillfully manipulated the market to fortify his wealth. His shrewd strategy involved seizing opportunities when others were selling, keeping hold of investments until others eagerly began buying. In 1929, he cunningly positioned himself alongside other struggling industrialists, empathizing with their plight while secretly taking advantage of their desperation. Krugler seized the moment to buy undervalued oil stocks from cash-strapped companies, swiftly acquiring Blue Pacific Petroleum Company and Tide Oil. Within five years, the value of these companies skyrocketed, establishing Sobek Corporation as the most dominant fossil fuel producer in all of America.

Expanding his reign beyond fossil fuels, Krugler diversified into aircraft and motor vehicle manufacturing, industries heavily reliant on his own fossil fuels. This strategic move afforded him the luxury of reaping the rewards from multiple sectors. Furthermore, the emerging advancements in plastics presented yet another excellent opportunity. While Bakelite and Celluloid had previously served as the primary synthetic materials, the 1930s saw the gradual rise of polystyrene, PVC, and nylon. Nylon replaced silk in the production of ladies' stockings, and plastics became an integral part of automobile manufacturing. The onset of the Second World War sparked an insatiable demand for plastic products, including hand grenades, tank parts and even components for the atomic bomb.

Being the astute observer that he was, Krugler foresaw this emerging market and capitalized on it. The United States government, recognizing the unparalleled potential of plastics, invested heavily in its development, providing over a billion dollars to private companies. Krugler's Sobek group secured a huge part of this funding, immediately pivoting many refineries to focus on converting crude oil into plastics.

Although there was a later drop in demand after the war, Krugler, drawing upon his millennia of experience and wisdom, planned meticulously for the future. Through an aggressive marketing campaign helped by an extensive media network, his companies began promoting and popularizing various plastic products that simplified people's lives. Plastics became an irreplaceable part of daily life.

Yet, the rapid dependence on plastics eventually exacted a toll on the environment. Accumulated plastic waste began polluting oceans, rivers, lakes, the soil, and natural ecosystems. Wildlife, flora, and human health faced unprecedented risks due to the alarming prevalence of plastic debris. Microplastics, resulting from the gradual breakdown of plastic waste, infiltrated food products such as fish, shellfish and even drinking water, creating an alarming entry point into the food chain. Mountains of waste, made up of Styrofoam, plastic bottles and bags, cast a shadow on the pristine beauty of our surroundings.

Inevitably, a global green initiative grew up in response to this environmental crisis aimed at curbing the production of new plastics, regulating existing technologies and transitioning to biodegradable products derived from organic substitutes. This shift posed a significant threat to the profitability and power of the Sobek Corporation.

However, Martin Krugler harbored a steadfast determination not to relinquish his ironclad grip on the fossil fuel and plastic industry. He resorted to extensive bribery and lobbying, funneling staggering sums of money to governments worldwide to secure their support. Krugler understood the growing challenge of countering the green agenda and propaganda, especially as distressing images appeared of baby turtles and albatross chicks suffering from eating plastic straws.

This constant battle between those advocating for a ban on plastics and proponents of the big oil industry plays out daily in the corridors of power. As in all conflicts, casualties occur, and Krugler would dispatch his henchmen to intimidate and sway politicians and climate change activists.

Occasionally however, Krugler himself would enter the fray.

That was why he found himself on a stormy day in Paris, France.

Martin Krugler was attending a critical meeting with international leaders at a climate change summit. He was there to face the looming shadow of the global green initiative, a threat that imperiled his power and profitability.

Draped in a pristine black tailored suit, Krugler made a resplendent entrance to the summit, where a cocktail of intrigue and apprehension greeted him. His notoriety preceded him. Whispers of corruption and manipulation crawled through the corridors, entwining with the chatter among environmental activists and politicians alike.

Commanding the main conference room, Krugler's keen gaze traversed the crowd, absorbing the presence of a diverse assembly of participants—from climate scientists to politicians, to activists and representatives from various organizations.

With finesse and authority, Krugler settled at the table, projecting an air of confidence that masked his identity as the ancient deity Sobek, cloaked beneath a veneer of charisma and guile. His knack for deceit had been his shield, a potent tool that allowed him to navigate the murky waters of politics and industry. He molded them to his will.

Within the crucible of the conference room, fervent debates raged. Krugler, a master tactician, listened intently, strategically calculating his next move to safeguard his vested interests.

In a calculated moment, Krugler rose to address the assembly, his voice a harmonious blend of silk and steel resonating through the room.

However, Anja Beck, an environmental activist and a staunch guardian of sustainability disrupted his symphonic address. "Mr. Krugler." her words pierced the charged atmosphere. "Your assurances of responsible practices cannot erase the scars inflicted upon our planet. Profit cannot take precedence over our collective home."

Though Krugler's facade remained unruffled, a glint of annoyance briefly flickered in his steely gaze. "I understand your concerns," he replied smoothly. "Yet we must consider the intricate tapestry of livelihoods and economies that rely on these industries. Practicality must govern our actions. Not idealistic visions divorced from the realities we face."

The earthy-eyed activist locked eyes with Krugler, her resolve unyielding. "Our world teeters on the edge, Mr Krugler." her voice unwavering. "We demand decisive action, not hollow promises veiled as progress."

A charged silence enveloped the room. the clash of ideologies cast a heavy pall over the gathered minds. The battle for profit versus preservation unfolded before them, the outcome of this summit poised to sculpt the destiny of the planet itself.

As the summit unfolded, the echoes of the storm outside

mirrored the growing turmoil within the conference room, a dance of ideologies clashing against the backdrop of an uncertain future. In the recesses of his unyielding heart, Krugler sensed the immutable tide of change, the groundswell of awareness against plastic waste and fossil fuel dependency mounting with each passing moment.

The pressure cooker of the global green initiative bore down upon Krugler and the Sobek Corporation, a reckoning on the horizon as the world stirred from its indifference.

As Krugler left the summit that day, his mind buzzed with strategies and plans. He understood that the battle was far from over and that he needed to protect his wealth and power.

Jacque Henri, a globally recognized green crusader, was a prominent figure in the conservation movement. He even won the Tyler Prize at fourteen for his campaign against plastics derived from fossil fuels. Now leading the Global Protection Initiative, an organization with a significant presence in governments worldwide, he was Martin Krugler's staunchest adversary. Jacque envisioned a world free from reliance on fossil fuels and advocated for substantial population reduction, goals diametrically opposed to the power and commercial interests of the Sobek Corporation.

As heavy clouds loomed, Paris embraced the mesmerizing beauty of the storm. Raindrops danced harmoniously upon the pavement, while the River Seine flowed fiercely under the turbulent sky. Guided by flickering lamp posts, Jacque strolled along the riverbank, happy about the day's meeting progress despite the rain. The inclement weather deterred others from the Quai Branly wharf, leaving the bridges cloaked in a somber gloom as rain tapped against the iron railings, creating a poignant soundtrack. Amidst the storm, Paris stood proudly with its monuments standing like ethereal specters. Wrapped in an enchanted aura, the city's narrow streets whispered secrets as cobblestones glistened like silver, reflecting the glow of ornate streetlights and elongated shadows. The alluring scent of coffee and croissants mingled, inviting drenched souls into quaint cafes.

As Jacque gazed towards the city's iconic Eiffel Tower, whose iron structure reached skywards as if striving to capture the bolts of lightning flashing across the sky, he had no time to admire the magnificent panorama. Suddenly, an unknown force flung him into the rushing water. Struggling to stay afloat, weighed down by soaked clothes, Jacque fought to fill his lungs with air.

"What the hell is happening!" Jacque thought, his eyes screaming with a terrified gaze towards heaven and the somber sky.

At that very moment, the river surged violently, concealing intense burning yellow eyes and a massive jaw adorned with rows of gigantic teeth behind a whirlpool of green scales.

A macabre patch of crimson momentarily lingered on the water's surface, a witness to the brutal force of Sobek, the Ancient Crocodile God, before the river's movement dispersed it into ribbons of flowing blood, streaming towards Paris's iconic monument.

Martin Krugler knew that removing Jacque Henri would merely be a temporary delay in the face of the rising tide of opposition against the fossil fuel industry. However, he needed time to find the triOsmium crystals that would grant him once again the supremacy over the world, just as it had in ancient Egypt.

CHAPTER 29

HOPE FOR A CURE

James Murray Jr enjoyed a privileged childhood, born into wealth and social status. His family had lived on their grand estate for over three centuries, a testament to their enduring legacy. One of their esteemed ancestors, William P Murray had changed the course of history with his remarkable invention, a flintlock that never jammed or misfired. The British army embraced this revolutionary firearm, catapulting the Murray family into a position of power and influence. They built a formidable weapons and munitions empire, capitalizing on war and conflict.

Tradition dictated that James would follow in his father and grandfather's footsteps, taking over the reins of the family business while forging a prominent political career. His father expected him to assume a role in the foreign office or to find his place in parliament. To that end, James attended prestigious institutions like Eton College and Oxford University. However, James had a restless spirit, and he craved something beyond the constraints of tradition.

Instead of immersing himself in the world of business and politics, James dedicated himself to the study of paleontology and biology. His burning ambition led him on adventures around the globe in search of the origins of mythical creatures that captivated mankind's imagination.

He looked to uncover scientific evidence to prove that these creatures had once roamed the earth or that natural phenomena had inspired the creation of these fantastical tales.

For James, the correlation between the Yeti in the Himalayas and the Sasquatch in the American Northwest hinted at a deeper truth. Similarly, he suspected a profound connection between the mysterious creatures of Lake Champlain and Loch Ness.

His days were a blend of conducting fieldwork in the Scottish Highlands, where he explored the depths of Loch Ness aboard his boat and delving into ancient texts within the hallowed halls of the British Museum. Every piece of information he unearthed brought him closer to solving the enigmatic puzzles that consumed him.

As time passed however, a relentless pain began to infiltrate James' existence. The agonizing headaches affected his focus, hindering his work and depriving him of the ability to engage in the activities he loved. Despite consulting esteemed physicians who diagnosed a brain tumor early on, no medical treatment or remedy seemed capable of alleviating his suffering.

James' father, the venerable James Sr, head of the family company and a longtime member of parliament, spared no expense in his quest to find a cure for his ailing son. Yet even he, with all his resources and connections, felt the tendrils of despair creeping over their family.

Yet, it was during one of the many high society cocktail parties that James Sr reluctantly attended that fate intervened.

Engrossed in conversations about the dire consequences of third-world expansion on global issues, James Sr found himself amidst a group of pompous politicians. Their callous discussions on conflicts and the necessity of thinning out populations for the sake of resources made his stomach churn and ignited a fierce unease within him. It was then that James

Sr's eyes met those of a woman named Jordan Garrett, who seemed equally disturbed by the discussion.

Without hesitation he turned to her, compelled to seek her opinion and a glimmer of hope in the face of such ignorance.

"Miss Garrett, it seems you disagree," he prompted, curious about her perspective.

"Well yes," she replied, expressing her opinion and making her disdain for such foolish ideas abundantly clear. To her, it seemed hypocritical, morally unsound and elitist to assume that death in underdeveloped regions, whether caused by famine or war, was necessary to preserve resources when the so-called advanced countries had already depleted their own.

"I have a question for you gentlemen," she continued passionately. "What will you propose if we completely eliminate disease, and human beings start living extraordinarily long lives? What then? Euthanasia?"

An overweight politician, clearly annoyed by her challenge, dismissed her statement arrogantly. "That's pure nonsense, science fiction!" he sneered, manifesting a derisive smile.

"Is it?" she responded, with a touch of anger in her voice.

"My company is on the brink of..." Realizing she had said too much, she abruptly cut off her sentence and walked away shaking her head. The group stood grumbling about how she had chastised them for their lack of respect for humanity. Their frustration lingering in the air like an unspoken truth.

James Sr could not shake off the encounter with Jordan Garrett and her powerful words. He sought her out later that evening during a lull in the party. He found her outside peacefully looking up at the moon and stars, surrounded by the tranquility of a rose garden.

"Miss Garrett," he called out, approaching her cautiously. "I hope I'm not intruding, but your words earlier intrigued me. What did you mean by your company being 'on the brink'?"

She glanced at him, surprise flickering in her eyes, before she smiled softly. "I apologize for being evasive earlier. It's just that what we are doing is quite unconventional and not everyone is open to hearing about them."

James Sr gestured for her to continue.

"Please, indulge an old man's curiosity. I find myself looking for something more than the trappings of wealth and power."

Jordan paused and gathered her thoughts.

"My company, The Garrett Corporation, specializes in cutting-edge research and development. We believe that advancements in science and technology hold the key to solving some of the world's most pressing issues. Our current focus is on increasing longevity and eradicating diseases that rob us of our loved ones. We aim to extend human life, not through greed or a thirst for power, but to grant individuals the opportunity to make a positive difference. Allowing them to explore, to create and to leave a lasting impact on the world,"

James Sr was intrigued by her vision.

"Had he found a way to help his son as well as discovering a purpose beyond developing ever more powerful weapons and personal ambition?" He wondered.

"What can I do to help? My family has resources and connections that I would be willing to make available to you and your company."

CHAPTER 30

SEEKING ACCEPTANCE

Like a nomadic wisp drifting through the sky, the Culebre dragon traversed the vast expanse of continents, finally finding a home in ancient China.

Nestled amongst the breathtaking beauty of the Qilian rainbow mountains, the Culebre settled into a sanctuary that mirrored its very soul. The rocks of Zhangye Danxia, adorned with a vibrant palette of maroon, magenta and lemon hues, towered overhead reaching countless feet into the heavens. Each crevice and curve spoke a silent language, paying homage to the rich history of the land.

With a head bearing magnificent feathers blending into the kaleidoscope of colors, the Culebre made a home within the labyrinthine canyons of this enchanting landscape. As the dragon soared through the skies, the awestruck people below gazed skyward, their eyes filled with reverence. To them, this resplendent creature embodied the harmonious unity of Yin and Yang, a captivating symbol of duality.

Known for its folklore and legends, China welcomed the dragon shapeshifter with open arms. The people believed that the Culebre was a divine being sent to bring prosperity and protection to their land. Embracing the customs and traditions of this enchanting country, the Culebre reveled in the rich tapestry of Chinese culture. Becoming a mentor and advisor to the villagers, guiding them through hardships, and celebrating their triumphs, the dragon shapeshifter used its ability to shift between genders to connect with the people on a deeper level, transcending the binary societal norms that often stifled its true essence. Utilizing its magical amulet, the Culebre created an extraordinary time of peace and prosperity. A ceaseless quest for acceptance had marked the dragon's existence, once driven away from the northern reaches of Spain by the oppressive clutches of organized religion. Countless countries had refused to embrace the Culebre for what it truly was until finding haven in the embracing arms of China. Their arrival here was a turning point. a reunion with a sense of belonging that had eluded them for ages.

Yet, amidst this newfound acceptance, powerful memories stirred within the Culebre's soul. It could not help but wonder about its soulmate and fellow Izbek castaways who had journeyed alongside in times long past. With its mystical purple amulet clasped tightly in its talons, the dragon sensed a haunting absence, a land devoid of its own kind. The Izbek had left long ago, but the echoes of their presence reverberated through the land. A marvelous sight revealed itself as the Culebre beheld the grandeur of the Pyramid-shaped Necropolis, an earthly marvel crafted from pressed soil and colossal stones. Behind its unassuming facade lay an empire of terracotta warriors, chariots, and majestic horses, all poised to go with Emperor Qin Shi Huang to the realm beyond. Ethereal rivers of liquid mercury wove their way amidst this magnificent army, casting a shimmering glow upon the walls. Constellations painted the ceiling depicting celestial bodies not even visible from Earth. Monoliths punctuated the landscape, adorned with intricate astronomical calculations, a testament to the knowledge imparted by the Izbek.

A question tugged at the dragon's heart. why had the Izbek departed this sacred land? Was it by choice or born of unspeakable tragedy? Had their companion at one time graced this land? Could one of their cherished crew mates now rest eternally within the triangular walls of the elaborate tomb? The Culebre's wings sliced through the air, carrying them across the expanse of this enigmatic land. As they soared amidst the echoes of their fellow travelers, the dragon could not help but ponder the mystery that had led them here, their presence an eternal enigma etched upon this beguiling corner of the planet.

Nestled high on the Loess Plateau in the heart of China lay the ancient city of Qingjian. Here, Yaodong dwellings carved into the steep hillsides offered relief from the summer heat, while in the winter months they radiated warmth from their clay walls. These dwellings, resembling arched structures sprouting from the earth, formed a majestic network of wooden ladders and stone floors, clustering together like the burrows of nesting Sand Martins along a riverbank.

Within this community, a young girl named Peiling Zhao blossomed. Born on the ninth day of the ninth month in the Year of the Dragon, she had an entwined connection with that mystical creature to which she prayed periodically for guidance. With her tomboyish spirit, she tended to and rode horses, outshining the boys in her village and the surrounding countryside.

As the Lunar New Year approached, a chance for change dangled before her in the form of a journey to Chang'an City.

Traders recognized Peiling's formidable talent on horseback.

They offered her family a fortune to apprentice her as a polo rider in the grand city.

Reluctant at first, her father eventually agreed, knowing this opportunity could lift his family out of poverty.

Although hesitant to leave the only home she had ever known, Peiling's excitement bubbled within her. The prospect of leaving the clay dirt behind and setting off on an adventure filled her heart with anticipation. Accompanied by her older brother, they embarked on their journey towards Chang'an, a city perched gracefully north of the Wei River.

Its majestic walls, moat, and canals evoked visions of emperors and royalty. The opulent buildings, temples, palaces, and pagodas touched the heavens, stirring amazement within Peiling's very soul.

As she weaved through the bustling streets, the diverse array of peoples from far and wide left her mesmerized. The scent of exotic spices and incense mingled in the air, intoxicating her senses. The eastern terminal of the Silk Road had brought together a tapestry of cultures.

Languages, sounds, colors, and smells intermingled harmoniously. In the heart of the city, the main square twisted into the form of the Big Dipper, an astronomical calendar etched into the paved stones, guiding the movements of time and destiny.

The Cien Temple complex, adorned with lavish hues of autumn, stood as a testament to the city's grandeur. Within its walls, Peiling encountered the giant Wild Goose Pagoda that seemed to stretch towards the heavens. This magnificent structure, housing the sacred scriptures brought back from India, seemed to her to defy gravity. The figurines of the Gautama Buddha gracefully adorned both the inside and outside walls, reminding her of her own spiritual journey.

The temple's sprawling gardens embraced Peiling with their abundance, a stark contrast to the arid highlands of her home.

Lotus trees, cherry blossoms and thriving orchards created a vibrant oasis, breathing life into her new surroundings. Monolithic stele stones etched with Confucian virtues and intricate animal illustrations adorned the gardens, fostering a sense of harmony and tranquility.

As Peiling settled into her new life, her unparalleled talent as a horsewoman propelled her towards her destiny. Serving her apprenticeship as a polo player and courtier at the temple, commissioned by one of the most powerful families in Shaanxi Province, she found herself competing in matches between rival families of immense significance.

Fortunes were gained and lost with the outcomes of these polo contests, where Peiling's skills promised victory and success.

Her days began at dawn and ended at dusk, consumed by rigorous riding training, tending to the horses' welfare, and the flourishing fruit trees and gardens. Guided by the Buddhist monks in her spiritual growth and education, wisdom and enlightenment infused every step she took.

Despite the demanding nature of her new life, Peiling cherished the opportunity. Becoming a skilled polo player was her path to glory and fame, a chance to break the boundaries that constrained women.

In a profession where gender held no relevance, Peiling's determination burned bright.

Peiling always marveled at the vibrant green grass that adorned the training quadrangle, as well as the colorful banners and ornate columns of the roofed cloister surrounding it. Topped with bright red earthenware tiles, the cloister looked particularly picturesque on ordinary days, with the banners gently swaying in the morning breeze as if waving their approval. However, on this specific day, the twenty sixth of January fifteen fifty-six, an eerie stillness hung in the air, apart from the reverberating commands of her instructor.

The morning's lesson focused on dressage, guiding the horses to reverse effortlessly and dart from side to side.

However, mere minutes into the session, the instructor abruptly ceased barking orders and fell silent. In the distance, a rumble began to build, growing louder until it reached a deafening crescendo. The entire quadrangle shook relentlessly, echoing like thunder, while the air itself seemed to vibrate with waves of destruction.

With a sudden violent jolt, the ground beneath Peiling's feet started undulating, resembling a tempestuous sea. The graceful horses bellowed in fear, losing their footing, and throwing their riders to the ground. The once mighty pillars of the cloister cracked and splintered, unable to withstand the force of the shaking earth. Bright red terracotta tiles cascaded from the rooftop, shattering on the ground.

Clutching the grass for dear life, Peiling was tossed and turned like a rider breaking a wild horse. Through trembling lips, she whispered prayers to her dragon god for forgiveness and pleaded for its help, fearing the collapse of her family's clay Yaodong home that could bury them alive.

The city itself seemed to roar with anguish as walls crumbled. The grand Wild Goose Pagoda sagged, and its towering presence trembled. The monstrous earthquake unleashed its wrath upon the land, tearing apart mountains and forming deep crevices. Rivers changed their courses, causing immense flooding, while candles danced like malevolent fireflies, igniting relentless infernos. The earth transformed, reshaping the once-familiar landscapes. Hills violently rose and valleys sank, becoming gaping chasms.

Streams erupted from the dry ground, carving new gullies, and structures that once stood tall succumbed to the relentless shaking. Huts, houses, temples, and city walls crumbled into dust, leaving shattered remnants of their former glory. Even the ancient stone steles, markers of an ancient civilization, lay broken in pieces.

As the tremors finally subsided, Peiling found herself miraculously alive, grateful for being in the open at the moment of impact. However, a sinking feeling consumed her heart as she realized that her family would not have been as fortunate. The hillside where their community lived had been reduced to a pile of rubble and despair, a tragic mix of clay, mud, and limbs. Only her father and brother had escaped the devastation. They were away from home when tragedy struck.

Amidst the chaos, the people of Chang'an and Shaanxi Province mourned their losses. People lit funeral pyres to honor the lives that had been lost, while the survivors started the arduous task of rebuilding their shattered lives.

The Great Wild Goose Pagoda stood as a testament to the quake's power, having lost three entire stories. However, the black obsidian statue of the Traveling Buddha remained steadfast atop its granite pedestal, gazing upon the Cien Temple grounds with a compassionate gaze, symbolizing hope, and resilience in the face of tragedy.

In a matter of mere days, terror once again consumed the already shaken populace as a magnificent comet blazed across the night sky. Half the size of the moon, its fiery tail resembled a blazing torch. This celestial spectacle foreboded more calamity, and to the people, announced the impending arrival of the Four Perils, instilling dreadful predictions in the hearts of those who looked skyward. The burning star dragon, along with the devastating earthquake, became a portent of doom. A punishment and dire consequence of humanity's transgressions.

Communities, their faith, and courage faltering, made the agonizing decision to forsake their once-revered protector, the Culebre dragon. Through the passage of generations, attitudes towards this mystical creature had shifted and now, emboldened, and unscrupulous vagabonds brazenly roamed, hunting the dragon with the sole intent of stealing their enchanted jewel.

Heart heavy with sorrow at this newfound rejection, the Culebre dragon ascended into the heavens once more and set its course westward. Guided by the ethereal comet traversing the sky, the dragon looked down with sadness upon superstitious travelers venturing along the Silk Road, their paths winding through the treacherous Himalayan plateau, leading towards the enchanting lands of Europe.

While Peiling continued her ascent to polo stardom, the Culebre dragon forever left her and the Chinese people behind, just as their fellow castaways had done long ago.

CHAPTER 31

THE MEDICAL MAVERICK

James Murray Sr used his influence to investigate the Garrett Corporation, uncovering its transformation from a humble hospital treating war-wounded soldiers to a global powerhouse in medical innovations. Spearheading breakthroughs not only in prosthetics but also in modern medicine, Jordan had daringly embraced the field of nanotechnology, aiming to unleash its limitless potential.

The irony was not lost on James Sr. The potential cure for his son's condition lay with a company that starkly contrasted his own business ventures. While his family's empire, W P Murray and Sons, prospered from crafting weapons of destruction, the Garrett Corporation's mission, "TO RESTORE THE SPIRIT" embodied a noble dedication to healing the wounds of war. With unwavering resolve, James Sr made a significant donation to support Jordan's groundbreaking research. Moreover, he enrolled his terminally ill son as a participant in an experimental procedure that would use the innovative micro-robotic medicine. He hoped to save his son while helping to herald the dawn of a new era in medical advancements.

As the day of the procedure arrived, the typically somber London skies stood in stark contrast to the monumental occasion that could revolutionize medicine. Undeterred by the dreary weather, Jordan felt an inexplicable surge of excitement. This was the day she and her grandfather had envisioned. The Garrett Corporation was set to propel medicine into an unparalleled future and solidify its position as a leader in reconstructive surgery and pioneering medicine.

In a modest laboratory, James Jr sat on an examination table. Jordan entered with the authoritative Dr Jeanette Han, a physician of Asian descent wearing a white lab coat and carrying a small plastic case. Over the past three weeks, Doctor Han had devoted nine consecutive nights to replicating countless micro-organic robots, using the original nanites stolen discreetly by Jordan from the alien sphere at the Hoover Dam.

A warm smile graced Jordan's face as she inquired, "How are you feeling today Mr. Murray?"

"I'm okay I suppose," James Jr replied, his voice tinged with uncertainty. "The pain comes and goes. I've kinda got used to it."

"Well let's focus on getting you better," Jordan responded eagerly.

Dr. Han stepped forward. She explained how they were about to introduce nanites intravenously into his body.

"These tiny machines will act as your immune system. We are hoping that they target and eradicate the invasive cells while repairing any internal damage," she explained pragmatically.

Though her face remained impassive, excitement churned violently within her stomach.

Jordan added cautiously, "James, you understand that this procedure is highly experimental. Nevertheless, we are extremely excited. Based on promising preliminary results we are extremely optimistic."

Shivering slightly from the sterile chill in the room and his understandable apprehension, James Jr nodded his head.

Without a miracle, he would not reach his thirtieth birthday.

Doctor Han retrieved a hypodermic needle full of a mercury-like solution from the case. Silvery specks danced within the glass syringe like trapped fireflies in a mason jar. She stepped forward and injected this living fluid into James's thigh. The room held its breath, uncertainty cloaking the experiment and its potential side effects.

The weight of expectations bore down on Jordan and Jeanette as they stood, fingers crossed in a silent prayer.

Time dragged on agonizingly as they fixed their eyes on James, waiting for any signs of change.

Would this audacious experiment pave the way to an extraordinary medical future? Only time would tell.

CHAPTER 32

THE HAUNTED MANSION

A looming manor house stood as a relic of forgotten darkness on the southeast slopes of Loch Ness. Its name whispered through the chilling winds, evoked images of evil and unspeakable rituals. Boleskine House, once owned by a notorious occultist and devil worshipper, carried a sinister reputation that drifted like mist over the land.

For years, the house sat vacant, its eerie presence haunting the nearby village. The arrival of two mysterious women fueled gossip, setting tongues wagging. These women, never seen in the village, sparked wild speculations among the superstitious locals. Some even believed that the two women held the power to summon the fabled monster lurking beneath the dark surface of the loch.

The history of the house intertwined with the ancient parish of Boleskine, dating back to the 13th century when a small kirk and graveyard were established. The clergy of the parish braved treacherous weather, traversing the desolate landscape on horseback or by foot.

One stormy night in sixteen forty-eight, a courageous minister found himself tasked with a macabre duty. Legend had it that two devious witches had raised the dead from their slumber in the graveyard of Boleskine, unleashing unholy chaos.

With haste, the minister battled against the elements, swiftly returning the animated corpses back into their graves. It was rumored that the manor house, constructed upon the site of the Kirk, had been consumed by fire, claiming the lives of all within. Locals whispered that this act of destruction was carried out by the vengeful witches, fearing the rising influence of Christianity.

Adding to the shroud of mystery that enveloped Boleskine House, whispered rumors mentioned a secret tunnel linking the nightmarish structure to the desolate graveyard. The existence of such a passage deepened the mystery, prompting questions about its purpose and the darkness it concealed.

Even today, the house instills trepidation in the hearts of the locals. The idea that anyone would willingly choose to live within its haunted confines is met with disbelief and concern. Despite not being known by their ancient names as the Morrigan and the Boobrie, villagers perceived the mysterious occupants of Boleskine House as either deranged or harboring a secret connection to the supernatural.

As the winds continued to howl across the loch and the villagers' whispers grew louder, Boleskine House stood as a dark testament to the depths of human fascination and the mysteries hidden within the ancient loch and the fabric of the land.

CHAPTER 33

A MASTER PLAN UNFOLDS

Ulf's eyes sparkled as he revealed, "We've discovered a store of TriOsmium crystals. We have an opportunity to replenish our amulets' true powers."

His words were laced with urgency and excitement.

Intrigued, Bouda leaned forward, his face glowing with anticipation, and asked, "Where did you find them?"

With a hint of secrecy, Ulf smiled. "At the bottom of Loch Ness in the Scottish Highlands."

Bouda's eyes widened as the implications sank in.

"Could a legendary monster be guarding them?"

His curiosity was tinged with a hint of caution.

Ulf's excitement was palpable as he confirmed that indeed, there might be shapeshifters protecting the crystals.

"The legends could actually be real." Bouda exhaled loudly and suggested.

"My company is currently constructing an offshore oil rig in the North Sea. It could serve as a base. It's only a quick helicopter ride from the coast."

A plan began to form.

United by their shared purpose, Ulf and Bouda were ready to confront the challenges that lay ahead.

With a mutual nod, the friends set their plan in motion.

Bouda organized the ship, and Ulf assembled a team of mercenaries from Sobek's security division. Despite the daunting task ahead, they were eager to face it head-on, resolute, and focused in their endeavor.

Shaking hands, they smiled. Once again, they would claim their rightful place as gods and rulers of this primitive world.

CHAPTER 34

A VILLAGE OF LEGENDS

Drumnadrochit sits on the north side of Loch Ness, a village exuding ancient charm and mystical allure.

As the sun descends behind the rolling Scottish Highlands and casts a warm golden glow upon the village, the air becomes electric with anticipation. Visitors from everywhere are drawn to this place, lured by the tales of the fabled Loch Ness Monster.

With its colorful cottages and the intoxicating scent of heather, Drumnadrochit stands as a place where ancient legends intertwine seamlessly with the present. It is a village where the threads of history and myth are intricately woven, inviting visitors to immerse themselves in its allure.

As the night sky unveils its sparkling tapestry, Drumnadrochit captures hearts and leaves a lasting imprint, forever carrying the whispers of Scotland's untamed mysteries.

Enriched with history and surrounded by breathtaking natural beauty, Drumnadrochit captures the imagination from the moment one arrives. Cobblestone streets wind through the village, leading to charming cottages that have their own tales to tell. With each step, one can almost hear the echoes of ancient warriors and clans, their stories alive in the atmosphere.

Standing majestically on the edge of a grassy cliff, the ruins of Urquhart Castle overlook the mystical waters of the Loch.

As remnants of a bygone era, the castle evokes images of chieftains and sieges, transporting visitors to a distant time.

However, it is the towering hill Meall Fuar-Mhonaidh that truly captivates the senses. The rugged slopes and craggy peaks of this hill offer stunning views of the surrounding landscape. On clear days, the panorama takes one's breath away, a symphony of nature's wonders unfolding before their eyes.

When the mist descends from the hills, a magical transformation takes place. The village, bathed in sunlight just moments before, becomes shrouded in mystery and intrigue. Ancient trees stand as silent witnesses while the tendrils of wispy fog dance around them, carrying secrets only the land holds.

James Murray, the young and ambitious professor of paleontology, rents a humble room close to the edge of this enchanting village. He finds comfort in the simplicity of his surroundings. The village, with its rich history, provides the perfect backdrop for his deep dive into the Loch's mysteries.

Having survived a debilitating illness, James feels a renewed vigor coursing through his veins as he prepares for an evening on the Loch, hoping for a sighting or sign on his sonar system that the Loch Ness Monster may truly be a creature from the ancient past. The professor aims to prove that the monster is a holdover from Jurassic times, specifically a plesiosaur, a mammal-like reptile and aquatic animal known to have lived in Scotland.

Every day as twilight paints the sky with hues of violet and indigo, James sets sail, his boat gliding across the mirror-like surface of Loch Ness. The familiar tranquility of the water envelops him, connecting him to the primordial past that pulses within this place. The village, now a beacon of warmth and comfort, fades into the distance as James ventures further onto the Loch, ready to uncover the enigmatic secrets that lie beneath the dark waters.

CHAPTER 36

ECHOES OF THE FORTRESS

Nestled beneath the vigilant gaze of the Scottish Highlands, along the graceful arc of Loch Ness, stands the resolute and awe-inspiring Urquhart Castle. Its commanding silhouette, weathered by the relentless march of time, bears witness to a rich tapestry of history and folklore that has unfolded through the centuries.

Constructed in the 13th century, Urquhart Castle has seen the tumultuous events that have shaped the landscape of Scotland. It became a battleground during the Wars of Scottish Independence, enduring sieges, and skirmishes as rival clans vied for dominion over the Highland realms.

Amidst the ancient walls, noble lords and valiant warriors shaped their destinies, their essence lingering within the aged stones.

Yet, it is not only mortal sagas that have left an imprint upon Urquhart Castle. Whispers of age-old legends and mystical entities meander through the ruins. Local folklore resonates with tales of the Boobrie, a splendid water bird adorned with eyes reflecting forgotten wisdom and wings carrying ancient lore. Enchantment swirls around the belief that under the shimmering harvest moon, the Boobrie appears from Loch Ness' depths, a sentinel of bygone knowledge and a conduit between worlds.

Within the shadows of this enduring monument, dances the Morrigan, a potent Celtic deity of lore. Revered as the Phantom Queen, she embodies a shapeshifter mystique, her presence both fierce and captivating. In the sacred ruins of Urquhart Castle, the Morrigan convenes with ethereal beings, dwelling within the Loch's waters. Their nocturnal gatherings beneath the radiant glow of the harvest moon symbolize a connection between dimensions, an unspoken exchange of truths and ancient rituals.

Whispers of a beast's existence resonate across generations, rumors of a creature gliding through Loch Ness' abyss with elegant stealth. Some perceive it as a sentry safeguarding enigmatic secrets beneath the murky depths, while others view it as a chimera blurring the lines between reality and myth, reflecting the enigmas shrouding the Scottish Highlands.

In the hushed embrace of Urquhart Castle's ruins, past and present intertwine, weaving a thread to the spiritual realm frolicking beneath the silvery moon's glow. As daylight fades into dusk and twilight blankets the terrain, echoes of ancient chronicles and the presence of supernatural entities softly reverberate among the seasoned stones. Here, history and mythology converge, etching an indelible mark on those privileged to tread these hallowed grounds and watch the quiet communion among the fortress, the Boobrie, the Morrigan, and the enigmatic Loch Ness monster.

CHAPTER 37

LONDON CALLING

The four wide-eyed teenagers—Miles, Sarah, Jose, and Ichiro—embarked on their first-ever trip to the United Kingdom with the Dana Hills History Society. They arrived in London eager to delve into its rich history and vibrant culture.

Their adventure began with a hearty English breakfast at a charming café in Covent Garden, where they relished sizzling bacon, eggs, sausage and steaming hot tea.

Energized to explore the bustling city, they ventured forth into the heart of London.

Their first destination was the city's iconic Tower. They paused to gaze upon Traitors' Gate, the entrance through which jailers ferried the condemned from the river to the execution site. Beefeaters, resplendent in their uniforms, patrolled the grounds regaling tourists with gripping tales from its storied past. Majestic black ravens roamed the fortress, their presence believed to safeguard England, perpetuating the myth that the realm would fall if they ever flew away. In the sanctum within the castle's protective walls, the mesmerizing beauty of the Crown Jewels captivated their senses. Each adorned item, from crowns to scepters and orbs, held generations of royal heritage and ancient rituals.

Bathed in the golden glow of the noonday sun over the river Thames, they marveled at the panoramic view spanning from Tower Bridge to the modern all-glass Shard building, realizing that this ancient city, steeped in history, continued to evolve.

Strolling along the scenic embankment, they passed the resplendent Saint Paul's Cathedral, a white-domed tribute to Sir Christopher Wren's architectural genius. Meandering through the historic lanes of Covent Garden, the tantalizing aromas of diverse cuisines wafted through the air from bustling eateries. Rhythmic melodies of street performers filled their ears. The vibrant allure of market stalls captivated their eyes. The city's atmosphere crackled with excitement and energy. Laughter and music echoed through the cobblestone alleys, enhancing the neighborhood's charm.

Their appetites whetted once more; the quartet ventured into a lively market. The aroma of traditional fish and chips and savory pies wafted from colorful and quaint eateries.

Every morsel was an ode to British culinary delights. Their taste buds rejoiced as they meandered through Trafalgar Square. Skillfully evading the flurry of energetic pigeons, they looked up and marveled at Nelson's Column. Blue sky and wisps of cotton clouds framed the naval hero on top.

As dusk fell, they ventured onto London's underground system, fondly known as the Tube. The rhythmic hum of trains soundtracked their journey through tunnels, stop after stop heightening their anticipation. From the vibrant streets of Oxford Circus to the trendy enclave of Notting Hill, they reveled in the distinctiveness of each locale and embraced meeting the welcoming locals. Along the way, they stumbled upon hidden gems, tiny pockets of enchantment not mentioned in the tourist guides.

Nighttime unveiled a dazzling spectacle of twinkling lights.

As they strolled along Westminster Embankment, the sight

of Big Ben, the Houses of Parliament and Westminster Abbey illuminated against the darkened sky evoked awe and admiration. Pausing to revel in the sheer beauty of the city's iconic landmarks, hearts brimming with joy and laughter, Miles, Sarah, Jose, and Ichiro joined by their schoolmates, took one last leisurely walk along the majestic River Thames. Sightseeing, historical walks and thrilling underground adventures, had filled their first day in the United Kingdom. It left them eager for more.

Standing open mouthed, they marveled at the towering London Eye slowly rotating in the distance, offering a breathtaking preview of their forthcoming adventure atop this magnificent Ferris wheel. Anticipation coursed through their veins for the next days adventures. They imagined capturing extraordinary Birds Eye views of the cityscape for their school blog.

Gazing at the enchanting city skyline, a sense of awe washed over each of them. It was not just the illuminated landmarks that mesmerized them; it was the shared camaraderie and gratitude they felt for one another. This unforgettable day had woven itself into the tapestry of their friendship.

As the first day of their London trip drew to a close, the teenagers bid farewell to the mesmerizing sights around them. Little did they know that London held countless more surprises and experiences in store for them. With wide-eyed enthusiasm and hearts yearning for new adventures, they returned to their hotel, drifting off to sleep, eagerly anticipating the enchanting city's offerings scheduled for the following day.

CHAPTER 38

A MENACING REVELATION

After helping settle the Squad and the Dana Hills History Club into the historic Piccadilly Hotel, David reached out to Jordan to arrange a meeting at The Wellington Public House on the Strand. The pub, steeped in old-world charm, welcomed them with its warm oak beams, crackling fireplace, and the melodious hum of lively conversations. The air was rich with the comforting aroma of craft brewed ales and hearty British fare, enticing passersby to step in and seek refuge from the bustling streets of London.

Once nestled into a cozy corner booth, David was amazed to see how much younger Jordan appeared than the last time he saw her at the Hoover Dam. However, she was restless.

Her fingers drummed anxiously on the table.

David sensed her unease. "What's on your mind?"He asked.

Jordan's eyes darted cautiously around the room, as if expecting some clandestine encounter. Once she was satisfied that no one was listening she began to divulge her thoughts.

"Do you remember the silver flask we found in the alien sphere back in Nevada?" she queried. "The one that caused all the commotion with the government officials and the men in dark suits?"

David nodded. The memory of that traumatic day caused a shiver to run down his spine.

"Well, the government officials failed to notice the slide on the electron microscope, and I managed to conceal it in my purse." Jordan revealed. "My medical company studied and reverse-engineered the nanites. Now we have produced many more. We can effectively cure cancer. Immunizations are obsolete and we have significantly extended life expectancy."

She paused briefly before continuing. "Unfortunately, this technology is incredibly expensive, which has caused many unscrupulous entities to come looking. They're trying to steal our research."

"Wow! Is that what all of this is about?" David asked, his eyes widening with amazement.

"In a way," Jordan continued. "As far as I know, American and British intelligence agencies are definitely involved, along with others who have more sinister agendas."

Jordan went on to describe how influential individuals, including royalty, government officials, and titans of industry, had approached her to get treated with nanites that would grant them near-immortality.

"Isn't that a good thing?" David interjected, puzzled by the conflicting information.

"On the surface, it should be," Jordan conceded. "These breakthroughs are extraordinary. They cured my cancer and gave me a new lease on life. But everything changed when I joined an elitist organization called the Global Protection Initiative."

Jordan went on to reveal how she changed her appearance using the micro-machine treatments. The promise of immortality had seduced her, and she believed that this organization shared her vision of making the technology available to everyone. However, as she became more involved, she uncovered a sinister truth that left her terrified.

"I simply don't know how far their influence stretches across the world," Jordan confessed, her voice filled with a mix of fear and urgency. She explained how the Global Protection Initiative, masquerading as global environmental crusaders, had a hidden agenda of drastically reducing the global population to preserve resources for themselves.

"They were complicit in the global COVID-19 pandemic,"

Jordan lamented. "It was a trial run, a test to see if they could get away with it. Everyone from bureaucrats to the media helped cover it up, ensuring the general public remained unaware."

David's shock was clear as Jordan continued.

"Now, they are about to unleash an even more deadly pathogen on the world, one engineered from the bubonic plague."

"The Black Death?" David exclaimed, horror stretching his eyes wide. "That disease wiped out three out of every four people in the Middle Ages. If manipulated through gain-of-function, the devastation would be catastrophic. Jordan, what do you plan to do?"

David leaned in; a sense of urgency etched across his face.

"Well, they are meeting in Scotland next week," Jordan replied.

"I sought the aid of an acquaintance in the government, James Murray, a Member of Parliament. I had previously cured his son's cancer." Her voice was tinged with concern.

"However, ever since I shared the information with him, he has disappeared. I constantly feel as if someone is watching me and I discovered my company headquarters ransacked not once, but twice. It's clear they are looking for the nanites."

Jordan's mind raced with thoughts of the hidden alien technology she safeguarded. She knew all too well the importance of keeping it hidden and she alone knew its location. "I suppose that may be the only reason I'm alive," she interjected, her voice wavered slightly.

"David, I can't deny that I'm really scared."

Contemplating his next move, David rubbed his tired face and pushed his hair back. His mind buzzed with the idea of involving Miles and the rest of the Squad. Their extraordinary abilities made them the perfect counterforce.

"Jordan, I might have a solution." David smiled, his voice steady with conviction. "I'm here in London for an extended period, and I have connections to people who can help us."

He paused for a moment, choosing his words carefully.

"This group has no allegiance to any nation or faction. They wield powers that can help, though I cannot divulge more at this moment. However, it would be helpful if someone were on the inside. Are you invited to their meeting?"

David asked.

"Yes, but I wasn't planning to go. I was hoping that the authorities would intervene. But it doesn't seem like they will." Jordan replied shaking her head, knowing reluctantly that she needed to head north to Inverness.

Jordan placed her trust in David. Their shared experience at the Hoover Dam had forged a bond of reliance. As she looked into his deep mahogany eyes that reflected the firelight dancing on the wooden walls, she recognized sincerity and refrained from prying for more details.

Instead, she settled into her seat, finding comfort in their friendship. They both leaned back, surrendering themselves to the plush comfort of their surroundings and ordered another round of drinks and some snacks. Eagerly, they caught up on the events that had unfolded in their lives since that fateful day in Nevada when their investigation into the enigmatic Ancient Alien technology had been abruptly halted by a sinister group of mercenaries. Though they had been deprived of their prize, they were grateful to be alive, unlike many on that dreadful morning.

Before parting ways for the night, Jordan hugged David and kissed him on the cheek, expressing her gratitude for his help and friendship.

"Thank you!" She exclaimed.

David smiled widely.

"No problem. See you in Scotland."

He reflected not only on the mission ahead but also on how much Jordan meant to him and the simple joy of sharing a drink together.

CHAPTER 39

HEAVENLY DISCO

C inaed Drake, the extraordinary Culebre dragon, had chosen to live in breathtaking solitude atop Mount Snowdon in northern Wales. In this haven, Cinaed built a forge and workshop dedicated to their art and sculptures. Within secluded walls, Cinaed crafted masterpieces depicting dragons in their full grandeur, displaying extraordinary detail and lifelike intricacies that captivated collectors from every corner of the globe.

Despite the comfort Cinaed felt in seclusion, there were moments when they felt compelled to brave the outside world and travel to London, the vibrant capital of England.

Situated within the swanky district of Mayfair, they owned a prestigious gallery which displayed their dragon sculptures with pride.

When Cinaed found themselves in London, courage surged within their being, prompting them to embrace the city's delights. Donning their finest clothes adorned with vibrant colors borrowed from the rainbow, they cast aside their shyness and embraced the exhilarating nightlife. Their destination: the celebrated Heaven Nightclub, a subterranean cavern where alternative lifestyles flourished, and individuality was revered.

As Cinaed stepped foot into the club, they were instantly overwhelmed by thunderous rhythms reverberating upwards into the foundations of the railway station above. A mesmerizing light show danced across the room, intertwining colors in enchanting patterns. Bolts of lightning darted across the space, echoing the dragon's long-lost ability to conjure electric currents and invoking its ancient power.

In this mesmerizing ambiance and amidst the pulsating energy of the dance club, a sense of unity and acceptance enveloped Cinaed, washing away past doubts. Their ethereal beauty halted club-goers in their tracks, entranced by Cinaed's grace as the dragon deity glided through the crowd.

Every eye followed Cinaed's hypnotic movements, their allure radiating undeniable magnetism. It was as if the air itself held its breath, intoxicated by their presence. In this sanctuary of self-expression, Cinaed found profound belonging, reminiscent of ancient days on Izbekia, surrounded by communal love and locked in a tender embrace with their eternal soulmate Hathor.

On the other side of the Thames River, Miles, Sarah, Ichiro, and Jose gazed up at the colossal London Eye. They marveled at the monumental metal ring holding observation compartments resembling giant capsules suspended in the sky. People said that this was the best vantage point to view the grandeur of the London skyline and capture breathtaking photographs. Little did they expect that their amulets, empowered with the ancient wisdom of the Izbek, would suddenly shine with intense brilliance. The Quad Squad circled on the Ferris wheel high above the river, their eyes scanning the city toward Big Ben, the majestic Houses of Parliament, and the iconic Tower of London. They wondered which ancient Izbek shapeshifter lurked below.

"Do you all feel that?" Miles asked, clutching his vibrant purple stone.

In unison, the Squad nodded. They all felt the electrifying presence nearby.

"What should we do?" Sarah pondered aloud; her voice laced with uncertainty.

Ichiro's face contorted with worry, his mind flashing back to the monstrous entities they had fought at the Hoover Dam.

"Is this shifter friend or foe?" He stammered.

Miles reassured them.

"I sense no malice here, only beauty and serenity. We must discover who it is and find out if we can help."

Exiting the towering wheel, the Squad called upon the power of their amulets, using them as divining rods to search for the location of the ancient Izbek shapeshifter.

Underneath the arches of Charing Cross Station, their mystic compasses guided them towards the entrance of the alluring club.

"We cannot go inside. We're too young!" Jose cautioned, a mix of anticipation and concern in his eyes. He suggested that the others return to their hotel while he waited. Smiling, he transformed into his hawk-like form and soared above the city, perching upon the eaves of the train station, where he eagerly awaited the appearance of the ancient Izbek.

Meanwhile, in the depths of the cavernous dance club, Cinaed lost themselves in the pulsating music, rhapsodic lights, and hypnotic rhythm. Unaware of the cosmic fate unfolding, Cinaed reveled in the evening's euphoria, their spirit dancing to the beat of London's energetic allure.

As the first light of dawn painted the sky in hues of amber and rose, the city awoke to the wondrous appearance of Cinaed Drake. Adorned in rainbow-colored garments and delicate feathers, Cinaed seemed like a living embodiment of a fantastical dream. Open mouthed and mesmerized, Jose fixed his gaze upon this extraordinary being. With an air of grace befitting an angel, Cinaed hopped into a classic black cab. Its tires kissed the wet asphalt, sending sparkling droplets into the air, reflecting the exuberance Cinaed brought.

Unfolding his wings, Jose soared into the growing light of dawn, chasing after this ethereal figure through the city streets. He passed Trafalgar Square and Buckingham Palace, until the taxi halted in front of the architecturally splendid Culebre Gallery.

Eager not to disappoint the Squad, Jose etched the street and location into his mind like a precious keepsake.

Returning to the hotel, Jose regaled the Squad with what he had seen. Their trip to the United Kingdom had uncovered an unexpected twist. With a shared determination, the team unanimously decided to postpone their visit to the British Museum. Instead, they prioritized a visit to the gallery to meet the ancient Izbek that now captivated their imaginations.

CHAPTER 40

THE DRAGON GALLERY

Upon exiting Marble Arch tube station, the Squad walked south on Park Lane. Expensive hotels flanked them on one side and on the other stood the magnificent greenery of Hyde Park. If Jose's reconnaissance earlier that morning had been correct, the building they were looking for on South Audrey Street would only be a short two-minute jaunt away.

As they continued their short walk, the swanky London art gallery began to materialize in front of them. There, they saw a beautiful sign displaying all the colors of a skilled artist's palette and the name "Culebre's Lair."

Upon stepping through the gallery's sleek glass doors, an opulent space greeted the patrons. The interior design was a harmonious blend of modern aesthetics and classic sophistication. Polished marble floors echoed visitors' footsteps. Tasteful lighting perfectly illuminated the artworks on display.

Showing the mesmerizing works of the enigmatic artist Cinaed Drake, this gallery served as a destination for art enthusiasts and dragon aficionados alike. This was a place where the fantastical and the elegant converged. The centerpiece of Culebre's Lair was a collection of stunning dragon sculptures meticulously crafted from metal and mounted on exquisite blue granite pedestals. Each sculpture captured the essence of these mythical creatures, with lifelike details and breathtaking craftsmanship. The metallic sheen of the sculptures reflected the gallery lights, enhancing their allure and mystique. One massive piece standing almost 8 feet tall, with sweeping wings and a head adorned with copper feathers, dominated the room. When the light struck it, the feathers gave the illusion of all the hues of the rainbow.

Large-scale prints and paintings that complemented the dragon sculptures adorned the gallery walls. They offered a visual narrative of the artist's connection to these legendary beasts. The juxtaposition of colorful and vibrant canvases against the metallic dragons created a captivating ambiance, enticing visitors to explore each artwork with curiosity and wonder.

Cinaed Drake's affinity for dragons shined through in every sculpture within the gallery. From delicate miniatures to large-scale pieces, the dragons appeared to come to life, ready to spread their wings and take flight. The artist's deep appreciation for these mythical creatures left visitors both mesmerized and inspired.

Culebre's Lair also offered a viewing platform where visitors could admire the sculptures from different angles, appreciating the intricate artistry up close. Knowledgeable staff members, well-versed in Cinaed Drake's work and the symbolism behind each mythical beast sculpture, milled around. readily available to answer questions and engage in thoughtful conversations.

As the Squad entered the gallery, their mouths dropped open in awe. They searched out the reclusive artist and when Cinaed entered the room, they were entranced by the artist's beauty. It was as if a vision from a fairy tale was standing right in front of them. Unable to talk, they simply admired the being before them, captivated by Cinaed's presence.

Finally breaking the silence, Sarah stepped forward, her purple amulet shining brightly. "Hello," she offered sheepishly. "My name is Sarah, and these are my friends."

She pointed towards Miles, Ichiro, and Jose.

"This is our Gallery," Cinaed replied, laying their palm across their chest, curious about what these children wanted from them.

"Wow, we love your sculptures. They are really beautiful,"

Sarah said, hoping to break the ice.

Cinaed, with a lingering smile on their face, hesitated to engage with the children or make eye contact. A sense of secrecy enveloped them before they saw the Izbek amulets and purple jewels adorning the children's necks. Curiosity stirred within Cinaed, and they mustered the courage to inquire about the origins of these mystical talismans.

"Where did you get those?" Cinaed gestured towards the alluring jewels.

Sarah glanced at the Squad before she responded.

"They were given to us by your kind."

With just a brief explanation, she extended her amulet for Cinaed to touch. An invitation to unlock its hidden secrets.

In that fleeting moment of connection, Cinaed understood the purpose behind the children's visit to their gallery. A wave of melancholy washed over them, regretting the missed opportunity of joining the Izbek rescue ship. Cinaed wondered if Hathor had been fortunate enough to return home.

"We are here to let you know that next time the Izbek return, you must be prepared for your rescue."

Miles stepped forward.

"For that to happen, you will need the power of your amulet.

When the rescue ship arrives, it will send a message guiding you on what to do and where to meet," he continued with conviction.

Worry began to consume Cinaed. Their amulet had lost its

luster and potency. The Squad however, offered reassurances, revealing information about hidden triOsmium crystals that could replenish the amulets' strength.

Motivated by the prospect of improving their chances of rescue and reuniting with Hathor, Cinaed agreed to go with the Squad on their journey to Loch Ness and the Scottish Highlands.

As the Squad shared their stories with Cinaed and explained that they were the direct descendants of the Ancient Izbek castaways – Huitzilopochtli, Bastet, Encantado and Kitsune.

They revealed that they had the power to transform into the avatars used by those survivors. Cinaed smiled nostalgically as memories resurfaced of their former shipmates.

When asked about their own preferred form, the Squad appeared astounded by the answer. Cinaed pointed towards the magnificent dragon sculpture at the center of the room, informing them that it was in fact a self-portrait. Stunned, the Squad struggled to believe that an actual mythical creature stood before them.

"Awesome," they all whispered in unison, their voices filled with wonder.

CHAPTER 41

ANCIENT ASTROLOGY

Hathor lived as an enigmatic hermit in her luxurious London apartment, never mingling within the city's social circles. Her reclusive existence served a singular purpose—she yearned for the day she could return to her true home on Izbekia.

Fate had other plans when news reached her that the Pharaonic Astrological Calendar, once housed in Hathor's cherished Temple of Dendera in Luxor, was to be displayed at the British Museum.

This incredible relic, depicting the Zodiac signs, awakened a nostalgic longing within her. Unable to resist the allure of Ancient Egyptian culture and the chance to reunite with her own handiwork, she made the decision to visit the museum.

With eagerness to reconnect with her heritage, Hathor left her home and navigated through the bustling streets teeming with modern life. Tall modern buildings interspersed with historic monuments stood like sentinels, their reflective surfaces catching the glimmer of sunlight as she weaved through the crowds. The city's pulsating energy enveloped her, a vibrant rhythm contrasting with her own timeless existence.

Approaching the imposing structure of the British Museum,

Hathor's anticipation swelled. The grand entrance beckoned her inside, promising a glimpse into her beloved Egyptian past. The air within the museum carried the heavy scent of history—a blend of aged parchment and the lingering echoes of countless footsteps that traversed its halls.

Walking past the exhibits, Hathor marveled at the relics of ancient civilizations in every gallery. Gilded sarcophagi stood proudly, their intricate carvings narrating stories of the afterlife. Glittering jewels, once worn by pharaohs, sparkled under the soft lighting, casting dancing rays upon the polished floors. She paused to admire a towering statue of Ramses, the great pharaoh who had left an indelible mark on her homeland.

However, it was the Astrological Calendar that had drawn Hathor to this place. Finally reaching the exhibit, she gazed upon the artifact with a deep sense of nostalgia. The image of Taurus, the symbol and constellation most intricately linked to her, resonated deep within her immortal soul. The carved zodiac signs, symbolizing celestial guidance that continued to intrigue scholars and dreamers alike in modern times, sparkled with a quiet potent energy.

Lost in thought, Hathor's memories were interrupted by the young voice of a curious museum visitor. "Excuse me miss, do you know the story behind this exhibit?" the visitor asked, pointing to the ancient calendar.

Hathor turned to face a young girl and three other young visitors, a gentle smile crossing her lips.

"Ah, the Pharaonic Astrological Calendar, yes indeed!" she began, her voice carrying the hint of ancient knowledge. "It holds the wisdom and connection to the stars that have guided our lives since time began. Each symbol, each carving, tells a story of the celestial dance that impacts our destinies."

Mesmerized by Hathor's presence and her words, Sarah Sirent leaned closer.

"Do you believe in destiny?" she whispered.

Hathor's gaze turned towards the purple amulets worn by the four listening teenagers and continued. "I believe in the intricacies of fate, woven together by the cosmos," she replied, with a broad grin illuminating her face.

"And as we stand here, gazing upon this ancient calendar, perhaps our paths have crossed for a reason."

Sarah's eyes widened, captivated by Hathor's enigmatic charm.

"That is certainly true," she said, turning to the other squad members who were nodding and smiling in unison.

As the light danced upon Hathor's magical amulet, its once faded brilliance began to stir with life. Fate had conspired to bring her into the presence of the Quad Squad. These descendants of her kin who also felt the magnetic pull of the museum on this remarkable day.

With a knowing smile, Hathor began to share tales of her long journey through history, stories of empires rising and falling, of love and loss. The Squad hung onto her every word, transported to a world where the boundaries between the past and present blurred.

In that moment, the sacred halls of the British Museum seemed to dissolve, becoming a portal to a time long gone.

Hathor, with her timeless presence and captivating stories, had summoned the spirit of ancient Egypt, casting a spell upon the Squad who were listening intently.

Her eyes, ancient and wise, reflected the knowledge she had imparted to her worshippers in olden days —astronomy, mathematics, music, and dance. Hathor's omnipotence had allowed her to guide and inspire generations, revealing the intricacies of the celestial bodies and the significance of the astrological calendar. Now, in this foreign land, she stood before the embodiment of her teachings.

Drawn together by a shared destiny, Hathor and the Squad found themselves united in purpose. The brilliant glow emanating from their amulets signaled to Hathor their sworn purpose to protect the world while seeking the powerful Izbekian crystals left behind by their ancestors.

Standing together in front of the Pharaonic astrological Calendar, Hathor revealed her premonitions to the Squad.

She feared that a looming danger lurked in the form of three rogue castaways.

Her former deities of ancient Egypt, Sobek, Wepwawet and Bauma seemed lost to the darkness of greed. They were in search of the very same mystical crystals, driven by a thirst for dominion.

Hathor swore once again, just as she had countless millennia ago, to protect humanity from the perils orchestrated by Sobek and Wepwawet. Their intentions, once again, threatened the fragile equilibrium of the world.

The Squad listened intently; their mission was now intertwined with Hathor's own. They had fought these rogue Izbek once before. They knew that they had to intervene and stop them once again.

United by their shared purpose of protecting Earth and recovering the crystals as instructed by the Izbek, the Squad geared up for the upcoming challenge. Starting their journey from London, they would head north to Scotland, where Hathor suspected the rogue Izbek were headed. Unaware that their mission would intersect with destiny, the group were drawn together once again by ancient forces beyond their control.

CHAPTER 42

A BEAUTIFUL REUNION

Kings Cross Station, an architectural masterpiece resonated with Victorian elegance and rich heritage.

As they scanned the grandeur that surrounded them, the Squads eyes widened with anticipation. They had no way of knowing that the station, with its soaring arches and timeless charm, was about to bear witness to a moment of unparalleled wonder. Two Izbek castaways, who had been separated by the unforgiving hands of time were about to be reunited. Hathor and Culebre, ancient beings of mythical origins, had each agreed to meet their newfound friends at the entrance to platform ten.

Unbeknownst to David, Bob, and the rest of the Squad, this encounter would transcend the boundaries of reality. These friends had been torn apart when they abandoned their stricken ship in orbit. Each soul descended upon Earth in solitary escape pods, scattered thousands of miles, and thousands of years apart.

This unique bond between the two Izbek survivors had flourished a millennia ago amidst the mystical depths and the communal crystal-green oceans of Izbekia. Then, as they traversed the vast expanse of the cosmos as explorers, their neptunic connection grew even stronger.

The Squad smiled broadly as Hathor approached, a beacon of ethereal beauty amidst the bustling station. Then, as if by some miracle, the crowd seemed to instinctively part before them, captivated by an otherworldly presence. The grace and unbelievable beauty of the Culebre now manifested itself in human form.

Curious as to what captured the Squad's gaze, Hathor followed their focused and intense stares to a being striding towards them with unwavering determination. Instantly, she recognized her long-lost companion.

The sheer force of emotions threatened to overwhelm her, weakening her knees, making it difficult to maintain her human form.

Overcome with an indescribable surge of joy, she rushed into their embrace, squeezing tightly, afraid to let go.

Their reunion transcended mere words; it was a silent convergence of souls—a moment that eclipsed the profound expanse of time that they had endured apart.

Tears spontaneously cascaded down reddened cheeks, a testament to the sentiment shared throughout the Squad.

Though they did not fully understand the weight of this reunion or the years of longing that had fueled it, the Squad experienced a profound connection to the enduring love radiating from the Izbek embrace. It was a love that gleamed like a thousand morning sunrises, casting a golden glow upon their souls. It shimmered like a thousand moons, their light dancing upon the surface of a tranquil sea. In that transcendent instant, the surrounding space seemed to crackle with electricity, as if the very air buzzed with an energetic joy on witnessing this extraordinary event.

With beaming smiles etched upon every face, they hurried to board the awaiting train. As they embarked on their journey together, driven by the thrill of the unknown, the everlasting bond shared by the Izbek castaways radiated a palpable warmth.

They were starting an adventure that would undoubtedly prove dangerous, difficult, and unpredictable when confronting Sobek and his henchmen. However, at this moment, it was a time to rejoice in the kind of love and camaraderie that defies the ages.

CHAPTER 43

THE ANCESTRAL SPIRITS

I f you venture from Nuuk, Greenland's largest city steeped in the enduring traditions of mixed Viking and Kalaallit cultures, up the Nuup Kangerlau fjord into the remote backcountry, a small tributary leads you to the enchanting Inuit settlement of Kapisillit. Standing sentinel over the cobalt blue waters, the majestic Sermitsiaq mountain looms overhead, its sharp ridges resembling knives slicing through ribbons of ice and snow. Gazing northward, immense jagged and crystal-clear glaciers cascade water into the head of the fjord, draining from the retreating Greenland Ice Sheet. Turning south, the landscape gently undulates towards the mouth of the bay, where scattered skerries guide the way to the Labrador Sea.

In this mesmerizing setting lives Aron Enoksen, an Inuit craftsman and artisan. His humble hut and workshop, hidden away in a quiet snow-covered alley, act as the sanctuary where he hones his trade. Through small frost-covered windows tainted with grime, a pitiful fluorescent light suspended from the ceiling dimly illuminates the room.

A narrow gap in the doorway welcomes the frigid Arctic air, casting a solitary shaft of light that creates the captivating spectacle of countless specks of dust dancing like delicate snowflakes. Inside, a lone stove valiantly tries to circulate a semblance of warmth. Metallic shelves full of an array of objects grace all four walls.

Aron is one of the last remaining indigenous and traditional artists dedicated to practicing the ancient craftsmanship of carving tupilaks or totems. To the Inuit, tupilaks holds the essence of "ancestral spirits."

These intricate figurines come to life in the meticulous carvings of animal teeth, bone, antlers, and stone. In forgotten times, even the bones of departed children transformed into ethereal sculptures, capturing their pure and innocent souls. These talismans would aid the Inuit in their battle against evil.

To this day, some Inuit commission their shamans, driven by supernatural beliefs and superstitions, to create these totems. Hoping to invoke their protective powers and vanquish their foes, shaman cast the totems into the sea whilst whispering magical incantations into the wind.

Aron now meticulously dedicates most days to crafting polar bear inspired tupilaks out of walrus tusks and bone. Through his skilled hands, the essence of these majestic creatures' morphs into everyday objects, such as rings, pendants, and bracelets. These works find their way to the traders in Nuuk, catering to the ever-growing number of tourists seeking a keepsake of their journey—a talisman whispered to channel the protective powers of their ancestors.

However, every so often, drawing upon his unique ability, Aron breathes life into a whale tooth, a rib bone or even an entire walrus skull, adorned with resplendent tusks. From these materials, he conjures hidden figures that materialize within his imaginative mind. Utilizing only traditional tools, he creates exquisite works of art, capturing the playful purity of centuries-old traditions— an homage to the rich cultural heritage passed down through generations. Aron produces no more than ten of these extraordinary pieces each year. These tupilaks are eagerly sought after by collectors who long to behold totemic depictions of both joyous and fearsome faces, enigmatic creatures, and whimsical portrayals of sea animals.

His true masterpieces, proclaiming the presence of Nanuk, the polar bear goddess, remain exclusively reserved for dealers who buy his work for affluent patrons in Canada, Denmark, and the USA.

Descending from an ancient lineage of Inuit hunters and Viking warriors, Malak Malaksen carried the spirit of Nanuk inside of him.

Recently, he had chosen to ship a crate brimming with Aron Enoksen's intricate sculptures depicting polar bears to Yorkshire instead of his London office branch at the Wildlife Foundation.

As part of a global initiative to reverse the declining populations of these majestic white bears, Malak's mission was to awaken increasingly apathetic societies to their plight. In his efforts to raise funds and amplify outreach, Malak intended to make these revered Inuit totems available for purchase during the upcoming symposium at the Yorkshire Wildlife Park. The Park, priding itself as the sole Arctic Ambassador Center for Polar Bears International in the United Kingdom, would serve as a platform to engage in open conversations about the art and the precarious predicament of these creatures.

Ever since leaving Greenland and his grandfather's teachings, Malak's singular goal had been to find a way to save the very beings he could transform into. To everyone who would listen, he preached his profound belief.

"We simply have to preserve these beautiful creatures and their habitat."

He stayed steadfast in his commitment to educate humanity about the peril these beautiful creatures faced.

The escalated global temperatures had caused their icy habitat to gradually dwindle, pushing them perilously close to extinction. Malak was painfully aware that the crucial solution lay in preserving the sea ice, a feat that would need a significant reduction in fossil fuel consumption.

Boarding the train for York at King's Cross Station, Malak started a journey that was destined to profoundly influence his life and his kindred animals.

CHAPTER 44

THE JOURNEY NORTH

As the train left King's Cross station, the Squad, Hathor, and Culebre settled themselves comfortably in their seats for the long journey ahead to Inverness. Excitement tinged the air as they embarked on an adventure that held the promise of danger, thrilling encounters and meaningful connections. Miles and Sarah's uncles hurriedly made their way in search of refreshments, eager to indulge in the luxurious offerings of the Pullman car.

While they embarked on their own mini-expedition, Hathor and Culebre, long-separated companions, found solace in one another. Reunited at last, they relished the precious opportunity to rekindle their connection, sharing tales that spanned countless centuries. Their love had endured even during their time apart on Earth. Their steadfast devotion never wavered.

As the train whisked itself away from the luminous streets of London, it passed over the Welwyn Viaduct, starting a breathtaking journey into the enchanting English countryside. The scenery unfolded before their eyes in a mesmerizing tapestry of rolling hills, where meticulously tended fields adorned with vibrant hedgerows and clusters of trees, danced in harmonious synchrony.

Suddenly, Miles, his senses attuned and heightened, turned to the rest of the Squad, a startled look on his face.

"Can anyone else sense it?" His voice carried a note of urgency.

An ancestral instinct informed him of the presence of another shapeshifter nearby. Hathor and Culebre momentarily interrupted their engrossing conversation.

They focused on their own finely tuned intuitions to see if they could discover what mysterious descendant was currently aboard the train.

Sarah's voice quivered slightly. ripples of uncertainty skimmed across her words as she asked, "Is it Sobek? Should we be afraid?"

Hathor shook her head thoughtfully.

"I sense no danger," she replied reassuringly and calmed their fears.

Determined to find out who or what was accompanying them north, Ichiro and Jose spoke in unison.

"Let's go find out."

Clasping their radiant purple amulets once more, the Squad followed the pulsating call of the unknown shapeshifter through the various compartments of the train.

Malak, thrown into a state of bewildered awe, sat rooted to the seat, his gaze locked onto the four unfamiliar children standing over him.

"Hello," Miles greeted him warmly, his voice laced with compassionate understanding.

"We are all like you and share a bond with you. Let me explain. His eyes shone with empathy.

Miles recounted the awe-inspiring tale of the Izbek, the narrative that had shaped and defined their very existence and purpose. He told of the hardships, revelations and extraordinary connections that had unfolded during their encounter with the Izbek rescue ship at the Hoover dam.

Malak, initially cautious and skeptical, listened with rapt attention as the Squad continued their narrative. They were desperate to convince Malak of their sincerity. But there was no way that the Squad could transform into their own animal forms on a crowded train. Instead, they led him back to meet Hathor and Culebre. They hoped that Hathor and Culebre could shed some light on Malak's ancestor, Nanuk.

As Malak listened to the Izbek's story and how his ancestor had arrived from space onto the snowy terrain of the arctic, a sense of wonder and pride filled his heart. He now knew his heritage. He was the direct descendant of an extraordinary being that adapted and overcame harsh conditions to survive. The Squad were almost certain that Nanuk had returned to Izbekia on the rescue vessel. That seemed very possible to Malak because it had been a while since the Inuit had felt her presence.

The Squad explained the urgency of their mission and if they were not successful it could lead to environmental chaos and disaster. As the train rattled along the tracks, Malak shook his head and ran his palm across his face as if washing away the disbelief. He always wondered why he was different and from where he had received his abilities.

However, he had no idea that there were others like him. He leaned back in his seat and recounted the purpose for his journey.

"I am on my way to a crucial meeting in Yorkshire," he explained, his eyes shining with determination.

"It's my duty to champion polar bears and raise awareness for their plight." He paused before continuing, "But once I deliver my presentation, I can join up with you all in Scotland."

The train glided into view of York Minster, its Gothic splendor piercing the sky, as the wheels came to a halt at the station.

Malak bid his farewells, hastily gathered his belongings, and disembarked.

Left with a moment to reflect, the Squad gathered.

Their spirits soared, grateful for such an ally in their ongoing battle against Sobek and his henchmen.

As the train chugged further north, leaving the magnificent Durham Cathedral and Castle behind, it traversed the glistening River Tyne, passing through a landscape dotted by industrial cities and quaint village hamlets. Crossing the majestic Royal Border bridge at Berwick-upon-Tweed, the train clung to the cliff tops, leading them into Scotland.

Gazing out of the window, they marveled at the tempestuous North Sea, its surface churned into a frenzy by frigid gusts of wind.

And then, like a vision unfolding before their eyes, the grand city of Edinburgh materialized, its foreboding castle perched atop a craggy hill, overseeing the sunken railway station nestled in the heart of town.

With the end of their journey approaching, the train carried them along the picturesque Fife coast, nestled beneath undulating hills cloaked in vibrant shades of green. As Inverness drew near, the landscape transformed into a more untamed and rugged terrain. A sentinel on the horizon, Dalwinnie Mountain stood tall and proud. Its peak adorned with a regal cloak of purple heather and the lingering remnants of winter's icy crown.

Finally, the train slipped discreetly into Inverness, and the Squad realized they were about to confront an old adversary once again. A sense of trepidation crept upon them, but they embraced the crisp, invigorating highland air, inhaling the rich tapestry of history woven into this remarkable place. Whispers of the ghosts of Culloden Moor seemed to flutter on the breeze. The allure of adventure emanated from nearby Loch Ness, with its mythical inhabitants beckoning them forward.

After Tossing their belongings into the trunk of a taxi they drove

westward towards the fabled Loch and their destined encounter
with malevolent and powerful forces.

CHAPTER 45

THE HOMECOMING

Izbekia resounded with profound jubilation as news spread that its brightest and best, believed lost forever thousands of years ago, were making their triumphant journey back home. Eagerly, families and loved ones gathered, their hearts brimming with anticipation as they awaited the return of the rescue ship. Departing from the shores of Lake Mead, the Izbek carried memories of their encounter with four extraordinary children, direct descendants of those who had been marooned, their destinies forever intertwined.

Navigating effortlessly across the vast expanse of space, the ship pierced through the celestial veil, passing nebulae, and traversing diverse universes until it reached the constellation Cygnus, their cosmic compass pointing them toward home.

As the ship slowed its pace and descended through the cottony embrace of clouds, the survivors' eyes widened with exhilaration at the recollection of the breathtaking beauty that awaited them. Massive volcanoes, erupting with iridescent torrents of violet lava, punctuated the landscape, painting the atmosphere with a kaleidoscope of colors. Their ethereal glow was juxtaposed against the backdrop of the sky and its six celestial moons, an awe-inspiring spectacle that had long eluded their memories.

Majestic mountain ranges reached towards the heavens, standing as guardians over arid deserts. These deserts, in turn, guided rainwater through intricate networks of rivers - forming an elaborate tapestry nourished by cascading waterfalls and winding streams, that flowed into boundless oceans.

They marveled at the adaptability of their bodies, quickly acclimating to the slightly higher ozone levels and gravity, granting them the strength to stand tall and take in the dazzling cityscape that awaited their arrival. Pyramids, obelisks, and wondrous dwellings caught their gaze, standing as magnificent testaments to their indomitable spirit. Their longing for these familiar structures had compelled them to recreate them as shelter on Earth.

It was not long before they effortlessly rekindled their bond with the citizens and the world around them, embracing unity, harmony, and the intrinsic interconnectedness of their existence. From the summit of the highest peaks to the most minute grains of sand, they once again found solace in their intertwined fates.

Upon their arrival, a symphony of celebration erupted. Tears of joy mingled with heartfelt emotion as families were reunited, their souls touched by the resilience and determination of those who had persevered through unimaginable hardships and returned triumphant.

Yet, amidst their own euphoria, a shadow of concern loomed; the realization that they had left some former friends behind, lost on an unpredictable world. With a heaviness in their hearts, the Izbek pledged to return, their resolve further deepened by a faint signal received from Achintya, a fellow castaway yet to be rescued.

Out of the 42 souls cast adrift on that nascent world so long ago, only 17 had made it back to their home world.

Without hesitation, they organized another expedition, driven by necessity and a sense of urgency.

The same ship that had delivered them safely home would now transport them back to the treacherous and ethereal planet that fate had intertwined with their own. Glowing with an otherworldly allure, its silver oval shape gleaming with rainbow hues that mirrored petroleum spilled on a wet floor, the ship stood as a proud testament to their ingenuity.

This once humble transport vessel for Izbek colonists, transformed into a dedicated rescue ship.

Upon stepping inside the ship, a mesmerizing sight unfolded before their eyes. A composite syrup coated the walls, displaying a captivating blend of blues and greens that created an otherworldly atmosphere. Embedded within this amalgamation were photosynthetic organisms intricately sustained by stored nutrients and an abundance of internal ultraviolet lighting. This ingenious symbiotic relationship ensured a constant supply of oxygen, allowing the ship's inhabitants to breathe freely even during the longest of voyages. At the core of this remarkable vessel existed a bubble of energy, a protective shield that enabled it to defy the limitations of space and time. Dwelling within this ever-shifting field of energy granted them the capability to traverse vast distances at superluminal speeds.

Cheers erupted as the Izbek once again set off on their crucial mission.

Their primary goal was clear - to rescue any surviving Izbek and, if possible, secure the triOsmium, preventing the crystals from falling into the wrong hands. Discretion and efficiency were paramount as they aimed to safeguard the delicate development of the young planet they encountered.

CHAPTER 46

VIALS OF HATE

As raindrops whipped and stung her face, driven by a northerly gale, Anja Beck stood on the deserted dock, her smart suit clinging to her drenched body.

A pulsating heart, fueled by adrenaline, quickened as her eyes darted furtively around the harbor. Anja, born in Copenhagen Denmark, found herself at the center of the storm, her instincts sharp and senses heightened.

Challenges marked Anja's early years. She navigated a world where her unique perspective clashed with societal norms. Diagnosed with autism spectrum disorder, she found solace in solitude and nature. Despite her struggles with social interactions, Anja discovered her passion for climate change activism, ignited by a deep-seated anger at the destruction wrought upon the planet by human hands.

Immersing herself in the fight against environmental degradation, Anja became a beacon for global youth, rallying them to challenge the status quo and demand change. Through social media and grassroots movements, she harnessed her influence to mobilize rebellions and protests, shaking the foundations of complacency. Her disdain for the older generations grew, fueling a sense of injustice and driving her relentless pursuit of a better world for all.

Anja's journey was one of resilience, defiance, and unwavering determination.

Traveling the globe, Anja attended Climate Change Summits, opting to travel by bicycle and sailboat to avoid vehicles reliant on fossil fuels. Embracing civil disobedience, she faced arrest many times. She stood with her disciples to block roads where petroleum tankers passed. Protesting defiantly, she splashed crude oil on priceless works of art.

As time passed Anja gained recognition. Time Magazine featured her on its cover, raising global awareness for her cause. However, some people became skeptical, concerned by the solutions she offered.

When she assumed leadership within the Global Protection Initiative after Jacque Henri's mysterious disappearance, she wielded unprecedented influence, shaping policies and driving substantial change.

Gazing over the vastness of the Moray Firth, a wicked smile graced Anja's countenance, foreshadowing a seismic shift.

Concealed within the approaching vessel were vials brimming with a virulent pathogen stolen from a laboratory controlled by the Sobek Corporation. These bio-toxins formed part of her sinister plan for global cleansing. She aimed to unleash devastation on the world's populace and prompt a radical reduction in fossil fuel consumption.

Envisioning Earth's rejuvenation and Mother Nature's resurgence, Anja yearned for the contented solitude she craved.

CHAPTER 47

A LOST SOUL

Doctor James Murray Jr set up his headquarters in the quaint village of Drumnadrochit, nestled near Loch Ness. In his relentless pursuit to unravel the mysteries surrounding the Lake's monster, he had transformed a rented house into his research center dedicated to paleontology. Moored on the lake was his boat, a Greenline forty cruiser he used to explore the Loch, aptly named the "Mystery of Scotland."

He had extensively customized this vessel for his endeavors. He fitted it with sensitive electronic sensors, a powerful searchlight and camera equipment. With its capability to function seamlessly both day and night, it proved to be an indispensable tool in his quest to uncover the secrets of the elusive creature.

When Doctor Murray received a dire diagnosis of an incurable brain tumor, he feared that his life and his work would meet a premature end.

However, the miraculous intervention of Jordan Garrett's nanites proved to be a resounding success. Within a matter of days, these microscopic marvels eradicated the diseased tissue entirely, granting him a new lease on life. He was completely cancer free.

Filled with a profound sense of gratitude, he eagerly returned to the Scottish Highlands.

On this particular night, the Loch exuded an eerie stillness, as if bewitched by its mysterious surroundings. The usual howling winds from Inverness and the Moray Firth lay dormant, casting an ethereal stillness. The moon bathed the tranquil waters in its silvery glow, creating a mesmerizing path of light across the surface. A delicate scent of heather wafted through the air, mingling with the earthen fragrance of the peat that painted the Loch in an ominous shade of obsidian.

Guided by peculiar and intriguing readings he had intercepted; Doctor Murray steered the Greenline 40 towards the heart of the Loch. His sophisticated sonar, resembling a commercial fish finder on steroids, had noticed a significant object circling a specific area of the lakebed.

Furthermore, his spectrometer and dosimeter ignited like fireworks, signaling extraordinary energy levels.

Suddenly a colossal thud shattered the tranquility. The impact echoed like thunder and sent the "Mystery of Scotland" careening violently sideways. Adrenaline surged through Doctor Murray's veins, his heart racing as he struggled to keep his footing. As the vessel teetered on the verge of capsizing, an unseen hand unleashed a torrent of water over its edges akin to a toy submerged by a child in a bathtub.

"Oh god!" he shouted. Urgency enveloped his straining voice. He pushed the throttle forward trying to regain control.

The boat quivered as its engines roared to life, battling against the formidable force that had collided with them.

Groaning once more under the intense impact, the boat seemed wounded.

Doctor Murray's heart pounded in his chest. Trembling legs led him to the spotlight, a mix of fear and determination gripping him tightly. With unwavering resolve, he directed the light towards the culprit. The beam cleaved through the darkness like a radiant sword, illuminating the chaotic scene. His breath caught in his throat, eyes widening in disbelief as an immense creature appeared from the water, its scaly, serpent-like frame glistening in the light. Eyes with an otherworldly gleam locked onto the boat as it circled.

"What are you?" Doctor Murray whispered in awe; his words carried away by the mist-laden air.

In response, the creature let out a deep rumbling roar, rattling Doctor Murray to his core. The sound resonated through the air, blending with the crashing waves, and echoed across the vast expanse of the lake.

The Morrigan, with her sleek and shadowy form shimmering in the moonlight, glided through the waters with a sinister grace. Drawing closer to the Izbek crystals, their mystical energy pulsed, casting an enchanting glow around her. She absorbed their power akin to a snake basking in the radiance of sunlight.

Transformed into a monstrous black eel, The Morrigan twisted with fury. The presence of the curious human threatened hers and the Boobries' closely guarded secret.

They could not allow the crystals to fall into the wrong hands; their amulets and strength relied on it, sustaining their vitality as they awaited salvation.

Without warning, the colossal eel rose from the water, its sheer size and power unfathomable. The boat quivered under the force of its monstrous head, as its jaws lined with jagged teeth, mercilessly crushed the cabin into a thousand splinters. The scene was a chaotic symphony of destruction and terror.

In a desperate attempt to maintain dominance, The Morrigan seized the petrified Doctor Murray by the head, her razor-sharp teeth sinking deep into his skull. With a swift motion, she flung him from the boat, leaving him mortally wounded.

As he struggled to reach the safety of the shore, thoughts of his beloved father and the unfulfilled desire to prove the existence of the Loch Ness Monster raced through his fading consciousness.

Lucy Gallagher lived in Inverness and worked as a waitress at a local cafe in Drumnadrochit. She had an athletic physique and captivating red hair with highlights of blonde and amber that resembled a crackling fire. Her striking emerald, green eyes stood out against her smooth alabaster skin.

A regular at the cafe, Doctor James Murray Jr was instantly captivated by Lucy's alluring appearance. Lucy in turn, found herself drawn to James, noting his ruggedly handsome features, characterized by whitish, slightly unruly blonde hair and mischievous blue eyes that exuded warmth.

Despite their differing social backgrounds—James hailing from a privileged family and Lucy being the daughter of a humble fisherman—the pair quickly formed a romantic bond. While Lucy harbored reservations about being accepted by James's circle, he reassured her of his unwavering commitment, disregarding any external judgments.

James, on a quest in the Scottish Highlands to unveil the mysteries of a legendary monster, stumbled upon something extraordinary: true love. Together, they believed in overcoming societal biases and planned a life filled with adventures, traveling the world in pursuit of mythical creatures.

After her shifts at the cafe, Lucy would wait at James's rented home. Typically, James returned before ten in the evening, granting them a few hours together before Lucy headed back to Inverness.

However, this night, with the clock nearing eleven and no sign of James, Lucy grew anxious. Despite her attempts to reach him through calls and messages, James remained unresponsive. Concerned, Lucy ventured out and walked towards the loch, hoping to find him.

As moonlight illuminated the path from James's home to the

dock, Lucy's unease heightened—the surroundings appeared deserted. Anxious thoughts raced through her mind about James's well-being, overshadowing the usual joy of their moonlit strolls together.

Just as worry threatened to overwhelm her, a solitary figure appeared near the loch's banks. Relief washed over Lucy as she recognized James, only to have that emotion replaced by alarm at his bloodied injured state and his unsettling demeanor.

Approaching cautiously, her smile transformed into a perplexed stare as she realized something was gravely amiss.

The battle with the Morrigan had extinguished his cerebral activity, his once vibrant mind snuffed out like candles in the rain. The nanites within Doctor Murray's body sprang into action, desperately trying to heal the irreparable damage. While his brain lay dormant, the nanites faithfully upheld his physical and motor functions.

Tragically, the encounter with The Morrigan's nanotechnology, transmitted through the bite wound to James' head, had taken their toll, causing his nanites to malfunction and forsake their original purpose.

Driven by a singular programming to preserve their existence and sustain their host's physical functions, the nanites underwent a profound change.

Eating for their host transformed from an exhilarating sensory experience into a mere necessity, an instinctual reflex triggered by a growling stomach and screaming muscles desperately in need of sustenance.

Craving nutrients to ensure their survival, the nanites led their host, Doctor Murray back along the shore. Seeking the path of least resistance, he was to become an unwitting predator, attacking other humans to extract the vital nourishment their bodies held.

Sensing Lucy's presence, the nanites coursing through his body spurred James to move with purpose, a marionette guided by unseen strings. Upon standing face to face with Lucy, his teeth bared beneath unfocused eyes. James began to gnash them forcefully, causing saliva to cascade from his mouth and pool on the cobblestone street. Terror gripped Lucy as James seized her shoulders and leaned in towards her neck.

Inexplicably, the monstrous incarnation of her boyfriend hesitated, granting Lucy a fleeting opportunity to break free and run to her car in a state of panic and tears.

Inconsolable, she sped away from the village towards the safety of Inverness and her father. Frantically fumbling for her phone, she dialed emergency services to alert them of an unwell and frenzied man roaming the streets of Drumnadrochit.

CHAPTER 48

UNDERWATER WARRIORS

Ulf meticulously assembled a team of three extraordinary specialists. Each had a unique skill set that made them formidable in underwater combat. These individuals outperformed typical mercenaries, embodying qualities of resilience, courage, and unwavering determination.

Leading the trio was Captain Declan Jones, a former Navy SEAL and seasoned member of the renowned Blackwater group. Declan's diving ability and almost supernatural connection with the ocean's depths hinted at the raw power he could unleash at a moment's notice. His chiseled physique, honed through rigorous training and many aquatic missions, mirrored the strength of Neptune.

Following closely behind was Lieutenant Kira Petrov, a former member of the esteemed Russian Wagner Group.

Kira showed tactical brilliance and exceptional ability to sense danger. She was an outstanding underwater marksman. Her keen intellect, combined with lethal precision and grace, made her a formidable soldier. Kira's piercing blue eyes reflected the infinite depths of the ocean, highlighting her unwavering focus.

Completing this formidable group was Sergeant Ron Sullivan, a battle-hardened veteran from the British Special Boat Service. Ron's confidence and experience commanded respect, with rugged features that spoke of battles fought above and below the water's surface. All three were masters of hand-to-hand combat, armed with extensive knowledge of martial art-techniques refined for underwater skirmishes.

The team shared a passion for facing oceanic challenges.

Years of collaboration had forged a bond of trust and camaraderie crucial for their survival in the chaotic darkness beneath the waves.

The cargo ship anchored next to the oil rig appeared insignificant against the imposing structure and the vast North Sea. A chilling gust of wind swept across the ocean, rustling flags, and causing sea spray to dance in the air. The atmosphere crackled with impending danger, as if nature recognized the perilous mission ahead.

Waves crashed against the ship's hull, their rhythmic roar harmonizing with the hum of machinery from the oil rig. The air pulsed with the energy of imminent action, as a sleek helicopter landed on deck.

The three mercenaries, dressed in dark tactical gear, disembarked from the aircraft, scanning the surroundings for critical details as they readied themselves for the treacherous mission ahead.

Each member meticulously inspected their innovative equipment, knowing their success depended on its reliability. Specialized diving masks with enhanced vision, propulsion systems offered unmatched speed in water and customized wetsuits ensured ease in navigating treacherous waters. Armed with spear guns and an arsenal of explosives, including depth charges and detonators, the mercenaries were prepared for any scenario. Each carried an Ontario MK3 navy knife, a Glock 17 semiautomatic pistol and the powerful HK 416 German assault rifle for land combat.

As the scent of brine and fuel filled the air, mingling with the acrid odor of diesel, the specialists mentally and physically readied themselves for the impending call to action. Their unquenchable thirst for the mysteries of the unknown drove them forward, unaware that their next mission would unfold not in the vast ocean, but amidst the enigmatic black waters of a Scottish highland loch, where they would face adversaries beyond their wildest nightmares.

CHAPTER 49

PRELUDE TO HAVOC

Martin Krugler and Bouda Napach traveled from New York and Cairo to Scotland in search of the elusive crystals. Upon their arrival at Glasgow International Airport, a sleek chauffeur-driven Escalade awaited to transport them to their destinations. Krugler was heading to "The Lodge," a prestigious five-star hotel overlooking Loch Ness. Bouda was to stay at the Aldourie Castle hotel, a majestic stronghold that had been leased by the Global Protection Initiative for a crucial meeting.

Meanwhile, Ulf Cadman chose to gather with his team of mercenaries aboard the ship moored next to the Sobek oil derrick surrounded by the turbulent waters of the North Sea.

In the ship's galley, Ulf conducted a crucial briefing for his soldiers. Despite his background in arid desert warfare, Ulf adapted to the challenges of the open sea, setting up his laptop on a metal table as the ship moved with the waves.

Their strategy involved using the Bell UH 1 Venom helicopter sitting on the ship's helipad to reach Loch Ness under the cover of darkness. Their mission was to land on the northern shore and dive into the depths to retrieve an ancient growth chamber protected by advanced cryogenic shielding. Once the crystals were in their possession, they would board the chopper again and swiftly return to the ship.

While confident in their abilities, Ulf emphasized readiness.

They may face unforeseen challenges, and they had to be prepared to employ lethal force if necessary.

CHAPTER 50

THE GATHERING STORM

The helicopter sliced through the crisp Scottish air, swiftly carrying Ulf Cadman, the enigmatic Wepwawet wolf, to a secluded clearing just north of the Lodge. Landing with a gentle thud, Ulf wasted no time disembarking, making his way to reunite with Martin Krugler and brief him on the mission.

Upon their arrival at Loch Ness, the ancient amulets worn by Ulf and Krugler glowed with renewed vigor, pulsating with burgeoning power. The crocodile and wolf gods now sensed the unmistakable presence of at least five of their long-lost Izbek comrades, accompanied by some other unfamiliar figures whose amulets emitted distinct and different signals.

Sobek felt an intuition that the meddling youths who had previously foiled their plans at the Hoover Dam would cross their path once more, sparking a glint of malice in his eyes and a wicked grin on his lips as thoughts of vengeance danced in his mind.

Never had so many Izbek gathered in such proximity since their departure from the mothership. The triOsmium submerged in the depths of the loch acted as a powerful beacon, drawing these disparate factions together like hummingbirds to nutrient-rich nectar.

Despite the growing number of parties converging on the Loch, Wepwawet exuded unwavering confidence in his team's ability to navigate anything that came their way.

Positioned as backup support, Wepwawet, Sobek, and Bouda readied themselves nearby, prepared to intervene as needed.

The chopper left the ship, marking the beginning of the operation at sundown. Ulf received crucial updates from Captain Deacon Jones via cellphone. They were on schedule heading over the North Sea towards the Moray Firth.

Quickly relaying the information to Sobek and Bouda, Wepwawet synchronized their plan. The trio arranged to rendezvous at the Loch just south of Drumnadrochit, selecting a secluded location where the dense woodland met the tranquil shoreline. Hidden amongst the trees they would hold a strategic vantage point overlooking the Loch while keeping them camouflaged.

Meanwhile at the Aldourie Castle Hotel tensions escalated at the GPI meeting. Discussions centered on the contentious topic of "Global Cleansing." Bouda ignored the ruckus, staying committed to Ulf's plan. He left the meeting just as the atmosphere within the room teetered on the edge of chaos.

CHAPTER 51

SMASH AND GRAB

D avid exited from the Wellington Public House. Troubling thoughts swirled in his mind after his meeting with Jordan. Her revelations about the Global Protection Initiative bore down on him, shrouding his thoughts in a darkness as profound and chilling as the fathomless depths of Loch Ness. Eager to convey the unsettling truths to his nephew Miles and the members of the Quad Squad, David was both surprised and reassured to find they had already been watching this group's activities.

Their suspicions hinted at something far more sinister— that GPI served as a haven for malevolent Izbek shapeshifters.

As they travelled north to Scotland, Sarah's uncle Bob strategically maneuvered the satellite over Loch Ness, preparing the Squad for their impending mission.

Their dual aim was clear: dismantle the organization's nefarious schemes and aid David in finding Jordan Garrett, who remained unresponsive despite their urgent attempts to reach her.

Miles spoke with unwavering conviction,

"Oh my god. The stakes have never been higher. If GPI succeeds, our loved ones, our communities—everything we hold dear—will no longer exist."

"They must be stopped at all costs."

Sarah nodded fiercely.

Set against the picturesque backdrop of the Aldourie Castle Hotel, GPI's clandestine conclave met to orchestrate and execute their malevolent scheme. Security-personnel kept watch, scrutinizing each entrant to ensure utmost secrecy and control. Guards stripped the attendees of their cellphones and keys, making them powerless and isolated from the outside world.

The global elites within GPI justified their dark agenda as unavoidable to restore the planet's balance, claiming Earths serenity had been shattered by humanity's destructive hand. Their chosen instrument of chaos was a devastating pandemic—a genetically manipulated strain of the bubonic plague—engineered to decimate three-quarters of the world's population. Their ambitions mirrored the biting winds that swept across the tranquil waters of the Loch.

Within the shadows of the dimly lit meeting room, Jordan Garrett fixed her gaze on Anja Beck, the enigmatic chairwoman and malevolent mastermind behind GPI. There was something about Anja's aloof and sinister aura that cast a shadow of dread over her. While lacking the means to contact David, she clung to a sliver of hope that he would come to her aid when needed.

With hushed whispers and secretive exchanges, the members of GPI, set their plans in motion. Operatives tasked with dispersing the deadly pathogen engaged in whispered discussions with Anja Beck, finalizing the logistics of their sinister mission. Their clear goal: to board commercial flights destined for remote corners of the globe and unleash the viral scourge, sowing chaos, and devastation in their wake.

However, unbeknownst to the assembly, a hidden presence lingered—a lone figure amidst the sea of upheaval. Ilsa Selch, the enigmatic Izbek shapeshifter and mystical Selkie, grappled with a profound sense of inner conflict as she listened to the harrowing discussions. Despite her crusade to protect the oceans, goals that seemingly aligned with those of GPI, the growing realization behind their intentions could not be ignored.

They aimed to amass power by monopolizing the world's scarce resources for selfish motives. Moreover, empowered by innovative medical nanotechnology, their families and allies remained immune to the deadly pathogen they planned to release.

As the moon cast its ethereal glow onto the hotel grounds, the Squad sprang into action. Navigating the shadows with practiced stealth, they infiltrated the hotel undetected.

Each step they took bore the weight of the world's destiny upon their shoulders, their determination swelling with every passing moment.

Inside the meeting room, an unrelenting tension hung heavy in the air, saturating the atmosphere with a sense of foreboding.

In a seamless transition, Ichiro and Miles transformed into their avatar forms, slipping into the conference room with utmost ease. Their eyes fixed on the table, they swiftly retrieved the coveted flasks, setting off alarm bells and resounding shouts of caution among the unsuspecting members of GPI. They stood in awe, mouths agape, struggling to understand the presence of a fox and a colossal black panther in their midst—a sight plucked from the realm of imagination.

Without hesitation, the fox and panther bolted from the room, racing through the corridors and out of the hotel. Bob and David stood ready, alongside Sarah, patiently awaiting their arrival. Above them, Jose soared high into the heavens and joined the Culebre dragon. His plea echoed through the skies, urging the dragon to intervene. As if a master of target shooting, the Culebre expertly swooped down, spewing fire from its mighty snout, incinerating the deadly viral pathogen contained within the flasks. In an instant, the dragon reduced the virus to dust, harmless and impotent.

With a firm voice dripping with determination, Ilsa stood tall, unraveling the sinister truth behind GPI's true objective. Her words pierced the convictions of the assembled group, planting seeds of doubt within the hearts of all who listened.

The air crackled once more, but this time it reverberated with the birth of dissent. Anja stepped forward to retake control of the meeting, but she was met by the stern and hypnotic gaze of the Izbek shapeshifter. Confronted once again by the insecurities that had plagued her childhood, she quickly backed down and retreated from the room.

As chaos reigned, the once-unified members turned on each other, their coalition disintegrating under the weight of the unanticipated revelations Ilsa had presented. Amid the ensuing pandemonium, the Selkie made her escape, leaving behind the Squad who had successfully thwarted GPI's plans, ensuring that their deadly pandemic would never be released.

Rushing inside, David anxiously looked for Jordan. He hoped to find her unharmed. Relief washed over him as he discovered her sitting on the floor, shell-shocked by the events that had unfolded before her eyes. Never in her wildest dreams did she imagine that a band of trained animals would come to her aid.

"Are you alright?" David inquired gently, extending a hand to help her to her feet.

"Yes," she replied, her voice tinged with a mix of bewilderment and apprehension.

"For now, at least. But I fear this won't be the last we hear from these deranged people."

"At least you're safe."

David offered a reassuring smile. Silently he vowed to seek out someone in law enforcement that could be trusted to investigate GPI, shut down their biological laboratories and distribution centers, and bring everyone to justice. The Squad he mused would in the future need to keep a close eye on any resurgence of GPI or similar groups.

As the Selkie departed from the chaotic meeting, she sought out her fellow Izbek, the Morrigan and the Boobrie.

She hoped to enlist their help and obtain crucial information regarding rescue.

CHAPTER 52

UNSEEN BY MORTALS

H idden deep within Boleskine House was a secret passage winding through the foundations. This mysterious tunnel connected the house to the desolate graveyard near the loch. A burial ground evoking darkness and superstition.

On this fateful night, just like many before, the Morrigan and the Boobrie followed the clandestine passageway unnoticed.

Meandering through the dark labyrinth, they floated like ghosts, staying undetected by the unsuspecting and sleeping villagers. Appearing as if by magic, the Morrigan and the Boobrie emerged into the stillness of the night. Veils of mist clung to the ancient headstones as the ancient shapeshifters danced between them, their ethereal forms shrouded in mystery.

With each step, their ties to the supernatural realm intensified, as the chilly wind murmured ancient incantations in their ears. Led by an invisible hand, the enchantresses made their way to the shores of the loch, where dark waters lapped against the shoreline. Nestled beneath a canopy of trees and shadows, a grove pulsated with ancient energy. Within this enchanted place, bathed in the gentle moonlight, the Morrigan underwent a metamorphosis. Her captivating form unraveled, contorting until she morphed into a colossal black eel, its sinuous body shimmering with latent power and enigmatic wisdom.

Simultaneously, the Boobrie, deeply intertwined with the land and waters, shed her ephemeral guise to become a monumental cormorant. Its majestic wings sliced through the air, casting colossal shadows on the ground as it readied itself for flight. Unseen by mortals, the transformed Morrigan dived into the depths of the loch, merging with its murky waters. As the Boobrie soared into the sky, the Morrigan continued into the unknown abyss. Together, they became guardians of the loch, their duty to safeguard the ancient Izbekian power emanating from its mysterious depths.

Unbeknownst to them, this very night would test their guardianship, pushing it to its utmost limits.

CHAPTER 53

BENEATH THE MOONLIGHT
AND BEYOND THE GRAVE

After thwarting GPI's malevolent plans and completing the first stage of their mission, the squad returned to the hotel to regroup. As night fell, the Squad ventured out once more, making their way towards the Loch to look for the crystals. Hathor and Malek had already taken up positions along the shore, their gaze fixed on the dark waters as they awaited the moon's arrival.

Meanwhile, back at the Aldourie Hotel, Bob and David checked the satellite feed, only to see a scene straight out of a horror movie. David's hand trembled as he gripped his cellphone. He needed to contact The Squad. Bob set his laptop on the table; his eyes locked on the screen. Images from his satellite positioned above the Loch and Drumnadrochit were displayed clearly. They elicited a chilling shiver down his spine.

Although the loch appeared calm and serene, the same could not be said for the village. Inexplicably, its usually tranquil streets were overrun with chaos. The residents, transformed into a frenzied mob, viciously attacked one another. Bodies littered the cobblestones with lifeless forms sprawled in disturbing disarray. Unattended homes stood with doors wide open, inviting the maddening melee within their walls.

The vessel that formerly was known as James Murray Jr had returned to the village after his encounter with the Morrigon.

He became an unwitting predator, attacking any member of the settlement he came across, extracting vital nourishment from their bodies. The nanites' influence spread through salivary contact. Those attacked fell victim to the same insatiable hunger. In no time at all, those infected unleashed a terrifying outbreak of carnage within the very heart of the once picturesque and peaceful village. It became a horrific place, where the voracious dead walked the earth.

Bob's grip tightened around David's arm as they watched this horrific scene unfolding before them. They struggled to understand the inexplicable sight of mortal wounds healing and fallen figures rising to join in the macabre dance of violence.

Adjusting the satellite's view, Bob's eyes widened as The Squad came into focus, walking briskly and confidently towards the chaos.

"David! Tell Miles what's happening in the village," Bob implored, his voice tinged with fear and concern.

"The kids need to be careful. See if they can find a way around the village and away from this madness."

David quickly dialed Miles' number as his heart raced.

Miles listened intently, acknowledging the update.

Something was wrong. He could sense it.

"Is there anything happening on the water?" he asked.

"We don't see anything unusual on the Loch," David responded.

"The danger seems concentrated in the village, and it's escalating."

Miles thanked his uncle and turned to his friends. A silent understanding passed among them as they prepared to move forward, knowing the unsettling events in Drumnadrochit had to be connected to the shapeshifters they were looking for.

Sarah hesitated, knowing she could not transform until reaching the safety of the water. Miles and Ichiro embraced their animal forms, readiness pulsing through their beings.

Jose surveyed the grim scene before joining the majestic Culebre dragon high in the sky.

CHAPTER 54

THE FIERY CRUCIBLE

A deafening eruption of fire and billowing charcoal clouds cascaded down the hillside akin to a pyroclastic flow. It surged towards the tranquil loch below.

From the stifling confines of this ominous cauldron, an awe-inspiring sight appeared - a majestic dragon, breaking the shackles that constrained it and revealing an indomitable power. As it soared into the skies, its colossal wings fanned the smoke, stirring it like a blacksmith awakening a fiery furnace with his bellows.

Adorned with resplendent feathers shimmering like a mythical rainbow, the dragon radiated an unwavering determination to help their newfound comrades. From its commanding heights high above, its magnificent silhouette partially eclipsed the moon.

Below, a scene of bedlam unfolded in the village, where friends now battled each other and families were destroyed, consumed by a ravenous frenzy that knew no respite. The villagers, devoid of humanity, clashed with merciless ferocity, trapped in a haunting trance. In a twilight state, suspended between salvation and damnation, these hollow vessels remained eternally trapped in the void of brutality.

Undeterred, the Quad Squad made their way through the twisted maze of streets, steadfastly moving toward the loch.

Guided by Jose from above, the Squad maneuvered cautiously through the madness of the zombified village.

Clutching their amulets tightly, they summoned their power.

Bolts of lightning shot from their very fingertips, defying the relentless onslaught, and carving a path amidst the chaos.

Fallen bodies littered the ground like defeated foes in a macabre video game.

With Sarah sandwiched between them for protection, Miles and Ichiro pressed forward towards the water. Terrifyingly, animated corpses closed in on them from the rear. And in that critical moment, the mighty Culebre dragon suddenly descended from the skies, its fiery breath lighting the path behind them, liberating those trapped in their unconscious state.

As the Squad reached the Loch, the Culebre unleashed its cleansing wrath upon the village. The dragon reduced the once-thriving settlement to smoldering ruins, as towering tendrils of smoke reached victoriously towards the moon. With this fiery crucible at their backs, the Squad approached the shore. They prepared to confront the collective strength of the malevolent Izbek, steadfast in their resolve to protect a world teetering on the brink of annihilation.

CHAPTER 55

FACING THE DARK DEPTHS

The helicopter's blades whirred into a slower rhythm as it touched down on the rugged shores of the Loch.

The three mercenaries jumped from the aircraft: the weight of their mission heavy upon their shoulders. The mist that hung in the air created an eerie atmosphere to the already mysterious surroundings. The burning village added to their trepidation.

"What the hell," exclaimed the pilot. The mercenaries however had no time to worry about what had happened on land. Their mission was in the water.

Captain Declan Jones, Lieutenant Kira Petrov, and Sergeant Ronnie Sullivan glanced at each other. A silent understanding passed between them. They adjusted their gear, ensuring everything was in place, ready to face whatever awaited them beneath the surface of the dark and murky loch.

As they walked down the steep hillside towards the water, the team could feel a presence, as if unseen eyes were watching their every move. A chill ran down their spines, but their unwavering determination pushed them forward.

Reaching the shoreline, they prepared for their descent into the depths. Declan conducted one final equipment check, his trained eyes scrutinizing every detail. Kira's hand strayed towards her spear gun, her senses tingling with anticipation. Ronnie tightened his grip on his combat knife, a grim smile playing at the corners of his mouth.

Taking a deep breath, Declan led the way, diving into the freezing waters. The other two followed suit, the cold shock of the Loch Ness waves sending shivers through their bodies. They cut through the water with grace as their powerful fins propelled them deeper into the unknown.

Blackness greeted them, its chilling embrace swallowing their forms. Visibility decreased the further they swam, the dark becoming almost suffocating. But these mercenaries were not easily deterred. They had faced the depths of the ocean before – this was just a different kind of challenge.

Confined spears of light from their flashlights danced like lasers before disappearing into the abyss.

Suddenly, a low and haunting sound reverberated through the water. It was a rhythmic yet spine-chilling noise that seemed to resonate from all directions. The team exchanged glances; their brows furrowed in confusion.

Something was calling to them, drawing them closer with its ominous melody.

As they followed the sound, their eyes widened at the sight that unfolded before them. Appearing from the depths into the light beams was a figure of malevolence, its skin shining and slimy like seaweed. The Morrigan, ancient Celtic goddess of war and death now transformed into a gargantuan eel snapped her jaws. Her luminous eyes pierced through the dark waters, emanating a malevolent glow.

Close to the water surface, the Boobrie, a large and fearsome bird creature, spread its wings, ready for an onslaught. The team had not expected such formidable foes, and their heavy armaments suddenly seemed inadequate.

Launching a precise barrage of rapid gunfire, the mercenaries began their assault. The atmosphere became saturated with the pungent scent of gunpowder as bullets sliced through the air and tridents through the water.

However, the supernatural enemies remained impervious to their weapons. The Morrigan effortlessly dodged the underwater javelins with cobra-like agility. The Boobrie soaring above, skillfully evaded every shot, before diving into the water. Bellowing like a crazed bull, she morphed into the water horse.

Despite their ability and formidable skills, the team found themselves outmatched. Their bodies collided with force, the sound of metal clashing against skin echoing through the water. Blow after blow, the mercenaries fought with unwavering resolve. As their strength waned, they clung onto the flickering hope of victory.

But the tide had turned against them, and as the battle raged on, the three specialists were overwhelmed by the combined might of their adversaries. One by one, their bodies succumbed to the darkness, their final breaths swallowed by the depths.

The waters grew still again, the silence broken only by the soft lapping of waves against the shoreline. The Morrigan, disappearing into the mist, surveyed the scene with a sense of satisfaction. She had defended the secrets of the loch once more, ensuring that the cache of crystals would remain hidden and protected from those who looked to exploit their power.

Unbeknownst to the mercenaries, their sacrifice had not gone unnoticed. On the shoreline, Hathor, Nanuk, and the Squad had watched the events unfold.

Despite knowing that the mercenaries had evil overlords, the Squad could not help but be moved by their bravery and determination.

Gathering their strength, they resolved to confront the Morrigan and anyone else trying to claim the Izbekian crystals for themselves.

CHAPTER 56

RESCUE IS IMMINENT

O n board the space vessel, the Izbek diligently assessed the reasons behind the limited success of the first rescue mission to Earth.

They pondered a multitude of possibilities that could explain why only a fraction of the castaways had been found. It was conceivable that some of them had willingly embraced their newfound solitude and forged a life on Earth, disregarding any calls for rescue. Tragically, others might have met their premature death. However, the most likely reason was that either they had lost their amulets, or the magical jewels had lost their potency over the extraordinary span of time, leaving them oblivious to the ships contact signal and the outstretched hands of salvation.

With precision, the second Izbek vessel settled into a polar orbit, strategically positioning itself to observe and map the planet below. As it traversed the Earth from its northern to southern reaches, the ship's steady rotation made it possible for a comprehensive survey of every square mile.

This time however, they held off on transmitting any signal until they had radiated the planet with a unique energy meant to recharge the survivors' amulets. Expectantly, the crew transmitted to the far reaches of the world below, desperately hoping to reach any survivors who still had these ethereal jewels.

Long ago, upon their arrival on Earth, each survivor had displayed their resourcefulness by leaving markers for their eventual rescuers. These markers transcended mere rock inscriptions on the beach of a deserted island: they were intricate and carefully crafted with profound thought.

Wherever they found refuge, they erected colossal megaliths, geoglyphs, and monuments, unmistakable evidence of their ingenuity, distinct from the works of the indigenous peoples. These sites appeared across the globe.

Some were buried beneath glacial ice or ravaged by relentless erosion, while others defiantly stood tall, refusing to be forgotten.

The grandeur of the Dendera temple and the temples of Crocodopolis along the Nile River in Egypt mirrored the sacred sites on Izbekia. Numerous other locations across the world, such as the revered temple of Pura Besakih on the island of Bali and the enigmatic statues of Easter Island nestled in the South Pacific, bore witness to the far-reaching impact of the survivors.

These beacons, served as sacred sanctuaries for those involved in their construction. Blue-faced druids would somberly assemble by the ancient granite blocks at Callanish in the Scottish isles or at Bryn Cader Faner, nestled near Snowdonia in Wales. At these revered grounds they celebrated and offered homage to the gods of nature beneath the gentle glow of the moon. Methodically placed, the circular stone rings acted as celestial landing sites, embodying the hidden knowledge and lore of the Izbek people.

As the ship continued its orbit, multiple transmissions began flowing in from the surface below. The survivors were directed to gather near their ancient structures. Then, the rescue vessel carefully descended, welcoming them aboard before swiftly returning to space.

Sensing a peculiar occurrence unfolding in the Scottish Highlands and a gathering of many Izbek survivors, the rescue ship held a stationary position above this ancient land, awaiting contact.

There was an inkling that a substantial cache of triOsmium crystals lay hidden somewhere in this realm.

CHAPTER 57

AWE AND TREPIDATION

Looking out over the Loch, Malek and Hathor waded into the water, their hearts pounding with a potent blend of fear and adrenaline.

Malek turned to Hathor, his voice quivering and hushed.

"Are you afraid?"

Hathor nodded, her eyes shining with determination.

"Yes, but let's be strong."

As Malek shed his human guise, the world around him seemed to hold its breath. The transformation that overtook him was not only physical but spiritual, a metamorphosis that awakened dormant instincts and ancestral arctic memories. The icy winds swirled around the polar bear. It chilled him to the core yet ignited a fire within him that burned with an unyielding determination.

Hathor's transformation was a symphony of unearthly beauty, a blending of ancient energies that twirled and coalesced, as if the very fabric of the universe took shape before their eyes. The celestial force that surged within her imbued each movement with an ethereal grace. Her eyes, radiant and otherworldly, held within them the eternal wisdom of forgotten galaxies. As the massive black bull's horns extended towards the sky, it was as if the very heavens themselves bowed in reverence to her cosmic power.

As they both peered upward, the Culebre soared into view, transformed in a mesmerizing display of enchantment.

With each undulation of their shimmering scales, the dragon exuded a magnetic allure that drew energy from the very air itself. Its wings carried them aloft with a majestic authority, commanding the skies and the gaze of those who beheld them.

As the dragon soared in the sky, the shapeshifters were joined by the Squad, who were struggling to recover after the violent encounter with the comatose cannibals in the village. Bent double, forcing air into their lungs, they stood on the precipice of another battle. Once again, the fate of their world teetered on the edge of chaos. Every breath held a sense of urgency, as if time itself raced against them.

Duty urged them to seize this opportunity to strike against the malevolent duo of the Boobrie and the Morrigan, now swimming in the middle of the Loch and preventing access to the crystals. The atmosphere grew increasingly foreboding, as dark clouds gathered overhead, obscuring the moon with an ominous cloak.

Hathor looked around at her companions, sensing the weight of their mission. She spoke with a firm resolve, her voice carrying a sense of urgency.

"We have to hurry before it's too late."

"Let's go," declared Sarah. "I'm ready."

Miles and Ichiro, their eyes gleaming with a feral instinct, nodded.

"Okay," Miles growled exuding the power of the panther ready to be unleashed. "Concentrate and be careful. Work as a team."

Sarah entered the water and embraced her dolphin form.

The weight of their mission pressed upon her like an invisible burden, tightening her muscles and quickening her pulse.

Suddenly a cacophony of distant howls and screeches from the wolf and the hyena, carried on the wind, served as a chilling prelude to the danger that awaited them in the depths of the nearby woods.

Jose soared effortlessly into the heavens and joined the dragon. The partnership evoked a mixture of awe and trepidation.

With their resolve firmly set, the shapeshifters were ready to confront the malevolent Izbek in the water and the evil creatures hidden in the trees.

CHAPTER 58

GUARDIANS OF THE TREASURY

As the harvest moon painted the charcoal storm clouds with vibrant hues of silver and purple, a sense of foreboding mingled with anticipation enveloped the air. Nighttime descended over Loch Ness, casting its dark shroud that seemed to rise from the depths of the lake.

From the murky waters appeared the Boobrie, its once-glistening scales now replaced once again by feathery wings that exuded a hunger for power. The Morrigan remained transformed into a sleek black eel, her eyes resembling polished obsidian, a picture of cunning and grace as she navigated the icy waters. Joined by the Selkie, the trio hovered above the shimmering crystals, crackling with transformative energy that pulsed through their enchanted amulets.

The Selkie, in her seal form, moved with elegance and strength on the water's surface, distorting the moon's reflection with each graceful ripple. The malevolent triad strived to guard the crystals that held immense power to shape destinies, ensuring that their potency remained exclusive to them.

Meanwhile, Sarah transformed into a sleek dolphin and ventured into the depths. Malak stayed along the shore as a steadfast guardian.

High above, the eagle perched on the dragon's back, surveying the scene with unflinching focus.

Sarah's silver-gray form shimmered in the moonlight as she navigated the treacherous waters, guided by the enchanting currents that whispered melodies of ancient power. With each agile movement, she drew closer to the coveted crystals, her eyes ablaze with determination as she neared her elusive prize.

As victory seemed within her grasp, a monstrous figure appeared from the shadows. Sobek in his giant crocodile form, stretching more than twenty feet long, snapped his jaws menacingly. The reptile's razor-sharp teeth glinted in the dim light, a chilling reminder of its deadly power.

Unfazed, the dolphin summoned all her strength and skill, gracefully evading the crocodile's gaping mouth, each maneuver a display of her superior wit as she outsmarted the fearsome beast. Seamlessly blending with the water, she managed to slip through its grasp.

In the heat of battle, the loch came alive, its dark waters swirling into a liquid vortex infused with an otherworldly energy. Sarah's resolve remained unwavering; her determination only grew stronger. The fate of the crystals, their immense power and the very balance of the world hinged on her success.

With an audacious and calculated final move, the dolphin deftly evaded the snapping jaws of the crocodile, swiftly gliding towards sanctuary with the crystals held tightly between her delicate snout. The otherworldly luminescence emanating from the crystals defied nature's laws, buoying Sarah with a mix of triumph and relief as she surged toward the shore where Malak anxiously waited. He urged her to go faster before their adversaries regrouped.

As the dolphin gracefully arched towards the safety of land, an electrifying sense of expectation crackled in the air. More ominous black storm clouds seemed to form out of nowhere.

Thunder rumbled and lightning flashed across the heavens, mirroring the clash of gods below in the loch. Amidst this celestial maelstrom high in the clouds, the Culebre dragon and the Hawk bore witness to the remarkable battle that unfolded before their astonished eyes. The Squad had placed their unwavering faith in Sarah, recognizing that she had the indomitable courage and unyielding determination necessary to confront the insidious shapeshifters and recover the coveted crystals.

Sarah gently deposited the crystals upon the sandy shore.

As if responding to some ethereal call, they instantly gave off a brilliant display of radiant light, casting an enchanting mercurial glow upon the faces of all those present.

This served as a tangible testament to the boundless magic and unfathomable power embodied within these precious stones.

CHAPTER 59

CHAOTIC WATERS

The Morrigan, Boobrie, and Selkie were determined to safeguard their powers, knowing that their abilities would diminish if the precious crystals were to leave the Loch. With a determined gaze fixed upon the shore, this malevolent trio pursued the elusive dolphin. Little did they know that Sobek, the cunning crocodile, had been attentively watching the unfolding events. To reclaim his own formidable powers, the crocodile knew he had to seize the crystals for himself. His movements mirrored those of the other creatures, as they converged upon Sarah.

Should he yield to his former shipmates and allow them to snatch the crystals and retaliate afterward against their betrayal? Or should he thwart their efforts before pursuing the dolphin? A lingering desire burned within him, a longing to finally exact revenge and complete what he had started at the Hoover Dam – to utterly crush, defeat, and consume his elusive adversary.

As Sobek pondered his next move, his thoughts were abruptly shattered when the massive eel's constricting coils encircled him, pulling him mercilessly beneath the surface.

An epic clash of titans was about to begin, as whirlpools formed like whiplashes, their iridescent purple lassos crackled with the raw power of lightning, creating a twisted gladiatorial arena where no mercy would be given. A chilling grunt of terror escaped Sobek's throat as his colossal form twisted and writhed, trying to break free from the clutches of the Morrigan. With each desperate movement, the dark depths of the loch threatened to swallow him whole.

Meanwhile, the Boobrie, the malevolent giant cormorant, sensed the imminent danger and ascended into the storm clouds. Its wings swept back and contorted, guided its evil descent towards the shore where Sarah, now back in her human form, stood with a mix of fear and determination in her eyes.

Undeterred by the chaos surrounding them, the Selkie displayed remarkable finesse, skillfully navigating past the entangled eel and the thrashing crocodile. Her face, the only visible feature above the water, kept an unwavering gaze fixated on the precious crystals.

Realizing the peril that threatened Sarah, Jose launched himself from the heavens, chasing after the cormorant with unyielding focus. His eyes homed in on the colossal black bird, talons primed for swift action. In an explosion of gusty winds that resonated like a thundering bullwhip, the hawk seized the Boobrie just as its beak poised dangerously close to impaling Sarah. Swiftly changing direction and banking back into the boundless sky, Jose protected Sarah from the looming threat. With a contraction of his powerful talons, he squeezed the life out of the cormorant before allowing it to fall back into the lake and sink into the dark waters that received its corpse.

Malek, now transformed into a majestic white polar bear, kept a steady gaze fixed upon the approaching Selkie. His honed predatory skills, acquired from the unforgiving sea ice and many encounters with seals, kept him poised as he waited for her arrival at the shore. With a powerful dive, the polar bear plunged into the loch and grasped the Selkie in a forceful grip. Despite the bear's formidable jaws and claws causing deep wounds, the resilient seal managed to evade a fatal blow, swiftly diving down into the depths with fear in her wide eyes.

Realizing the futility of the battle and understanding that the crystals were not her priority, the Selkie wisely chose discretion over valor. Swiftly she swam away vowing to return to the safety of the vast ocean, relying on the mysterious nanites within her veins to heal her wounds and restore her elegant form. Disappointed at missing his chance for victory, the polar bear paced back and forth like a thwarted soldier, eager for a second opportunity to confront his elusive adversary.

As the tranquil waters of the loch settled, a heavy silence enveloped the scene. The faint ripples on the surface concealed the recent intense clashes beneath the water's surface. Suddenly breaking the stillness, a massive black head appeared from the depths, unleashing a cascade of waves towards the shore. An endless expanse of charcoal coils trailed behind, revealing the Morrigan, her eyes fixed on Sarah; the solitary figure standing alone. With sinister grace, the Morrigan swiftly slithered towards the shore like a sidewinding snake, her focus set on the coveted crystals.

Sarah, clutching her amulet, conjured lightning from the storm clouds.

With eerie agility, the Morrigan swiftly evaded the onslaught, using her own jewel to absorb the powerful energy hurtling towards her. The menacing eel closed in on Sarah, its immense form rising from the water. Towering twenty feet above the surface, its ugly head poised ready to strike. Summoning the last reserves of her courage, Sarah unleashed one final burst of crackling energy from her palms, desperate to survive. With her Heart pounding against her ribcage, she turned and sprinted away, sheer terror flooding her veins. Each strained breath left her bracing for the monster's attack, convinced that her very body would be swept up by the impending doom overhead.

As the Morrigans neck snapped forcefully forward and down,

Sarah was in grave danger.

Suddenly swooping from the sky, the Culebre dragon in a cloud of smoke and fire slammed their claws forward and grabbed the long body of the monstrous eel. Just in time, the dragon diverted the eel's snapping jaws and razor-like teeth away from Sarah's frail body as the teen threw herself to the ground. Rising majestically towards the dark clouds backlighted by thunderclaps, the dragon carried the eel like a trophy over the center of the loch. Summoning all the energy to its amulet the dragon let its adversary fall before unleashing a stream of fire that totally engulfed the eel.

As her body cooked and her flesh melted, the screams of the Morrigan echoed through the valley and rushed over the surface of the loch before ascending the steep peat slopes to rebound back off the heather-covered summits.

As the chaotic waters settled, serene ripples spread in circular motion across the expansive Loch. The defeated Morrigan, engulfed in steam, descended into the depths, sinking to a resting place where the crystals had once shimmered.

Malak and Jose quickly resumed their human forms. With concern etched on their faces, they rushed to Sarah's side.

"Are you alright?" They asked.

Sarah, though visibly shaken, gazed back at them, her widened eyes reflecting the determination of her spirit.

"I think so. That was a close call," she replied, her voice wavering with relief.

With lingering adrenaline coursing through her veins, she shook off the remnants of fear. Glancing around, she

furtively scanned the Loch to ensure her adversaries were not about to return.

In a gesture of gratitude and reverence, Sarah looked up at the sky. With a genuine smile, she clasped her hands together, offering a bow of gratitude towards the Culebre dragon that had swooped down to save her.

In that moment, she knew the dragon had rescued her from a dreadful fate.

Returning her focus to Malak and Jose, Sarah's eyes radiated with determination once more.

"We must find Miles, Ichiro, and Hathor. They too are in danger and need our help."

CHAPTER 60

THE BATTLE RESUMES

The moon vanished behind the tumultuous storm clouds, darkening the pathways under the thick canopy of trees. With their eyes glowing with feral instincts, Miles and Ichiro transformed into the majestic panther and the nimble fox, blending with the shadows.

Followed by Hathor, they silently vanished into the depths of the forest.

In the looming darkness, unseen eyes followed their every move, ancient spirits cackling with wicked delight. The wolf and the hyena lurked in the shadows, ready to seize the crystals for themselves. Their amulets glimmered with resurrected power, recharged with formidable strength since their arrival in this remote part of Scotland.

Ulf knew the size of the challenge that lay before him. Eight equally formidable opponents stood in his path, each having unwavering strength. To prevail, he needed not only a cunning strategy to outwit them with a special demise reserved for the meddling kids who had foiled him at the Hoover Dam.

The panther and the wolf were about to rekindle their unfinished duel, engaging once again in a frenzied dance of teeth and claws.

Sensing that the malevolent Izbek were close, the air was thick with anticipation as Miles, Ichiro, and Hathor prepared for battle. They moved into a dense thicket of ancient trees.

They knew that Wepwawet and Bouda, consumed by their thirst for power, wanted to get their hands on the triOsmium that held the key to their return to dominance over this world.

Miles, his muscles rippling beneath the sleek black coat of the panther, prowled silently, his senses heightened. Ichiro, his russet fur standing on end, immersed himself as the fox.

His eyes were gleaming with determination. And Hathor, resplendent in her majestic bull form, exuded an aura of strength and nobility as she surveyed the battleground.

In the heart of the trees, tucked away from prying eyes, Wepwawet and Bouda waited in ambush, their devious smiles belying their malicious intentions. With eyes keen like the wolf, Wepwawet's grey fur camouflaged his dark presence in the undergrowth. Bouda, his hyena avatar a twisted mockery of nature, bared his jagged teeth in a menacing grin.

As the combatants came face to face, the battle began. A clash of fangs and claws erupted. Miles sprang forward with the grace of a hunting cat, landing a fierce blow on Wepwawet's flank, while Ichiro darted and weaved, delivering swift bites to the Hyena's hide. Hathor charged forward; her massive horns poised to strike a devastating blow. Their bodies moved with deadly elegance, sleek muscles rippling beneath their coats as they fought for dominance.

The scent of blood and primal sweat filled the air, mingling with the acrid smell of singed fur as their bodies collided with ferocious intensity. The thicket erupted in a whirlwind of flying fur and leaves. The battle was not limited to their animal forms alone. Each combatant's ethereal amulet pulsated with energy. With a flicker of electricity, they summoned the power within, conjuring bolts of purple lightning that crackled through the air. The clash of elemental forces intensified, transforming the battlefield into a symphony of noise and dazzling spectacle.

Rolling like interlocked dervishes the maelstrom of fighters spilled out of the woods, across a ribbon of meadow and into the confines of the worn stone walls of Urquhart Castle.

Thunderclaps shook the sky and flashes of lightning intermittently illuminated the moss-covered stones, mirroring the drama unfolding on the ground. The ancient echoes of past battles mingling with the furious roars and growls of the combatants. The castle, a silent observer to countless historical events, now bore witness to a cataclysmic clash between ancient forces.

For hours, they fought with unwavering determination, the air thick with the scent of blood and the lingering taste of electrical energy. The ruined walls, damp from the mist, reflected the incandescent light of the amulets' power as a denser fog, now rolling in from the lake, glowed around the warring shapeshifters. Hathor, wielding her horns like dual Daisho blades, managed to land maiming blows to the Hyena and the wolf while the fox and the panther closed in.

Desperation filled the malevolent beings as they realized their chances of seizing the coveted crystals were slipping away.

With each strike and counterattack, the air crackled with energy. The ancient trees whispered secrets and offered their support, their branches extending and entwining to create obstacles for the malevolent duo.

But Wepwawet and Bouda were not easily defeated. They fought back with ferocity and cunning, their eyes gleaming with hatred and the hunger for domination. Wepwawet used his agility to dodge Miles' attacks, retaliating with lightning-fast slashes, while Bouda's twisted form allowed him to unleash a barrage of savage bites and nips.

Undeterred, Miles, Ichiro, and Hathor rallied together, melding their individual strengths into a unified force. Miles used his speed and stealth to flank Wepwawet his sharp claws slashing through silver fur. Ichiro, nimble and quick-witted, distracted Bouda, allowing Hathor's mighty horns to find their mark, sending the were-hyena sprawling.

As the battle raged on, the malevolent duo grew weary, their once-confident grins replaced with expressions of desperation.

Finally, with one final surge of strength, Miles pounced on Wepwawet, delivering a bone-crushing blow, while Ichiro skillfully immobilized Bouda, his jaws clamped around the hyena's throat. Hathor, with a triumphant bellow, unleashed a surge of primal fury.

In a final, thunderous collision of wills, the Squad once again emerged victorious. Wepwawet and Bouda, battered and beaten, retreated, back into the thicket and disappeared amidst the dense trees, their dreams of ultimate power shattered.

Sensing that Sobek would not be meeting them they took refuge waiting for dawn. Miles, Ichiro, and Hathor bruised yet unbroken hurried to meet Sarah and Malek who were guarding the crystals at the waters edge.

"Is it just me or are the crystals vibrating?"

Miles asked noticing that the very ground seemed to tremble and shiver.

Hathor looked worried, a sense of urgency on her face.

"We need to get the crystals back to the bottom of the lake.

They need to be kept cold or this entire valley and most of Scotland will no longer exist. We will be blown to tiny little pieces."

Sarah once again took charge of the crystals and transformed into the sleek and agile dolphin. With rapid and powerful strokes of her tail Sarah dived to the bottom of the inky loch and sequestered the crystals in their cryogenic growth chamber back into their ancient resting place. Safe for now the crystals posed no threat.

As the Dragon and the hawk descended from the stormy sky and landed in front of Urquhart Castle, the echoes of the clash lingered, a testament to the enduring power of courage and the eternal struggle between good and evil.

CHAPTER 61

SMOKE RISES

Hathor and the Culebre together embraced each member of the Squad. They owed them a great debt of gratitude.

No longer apart and their souls once more intertwined, Hathor and the Culebre found solace in each other's endearing love. Embracing their role as the Ancient Izbek, they accepted the solemn duty of protecting the precious crystals. The power pulsated within their ancient amulets, artifacts resonating with dormant energy, as they called upon their magic to summon the hidden treasures from the depths of Loch Ness. The mystical sight of the crystals materializing before them was awe-inspiring, and they understood the urgent need to safeguard them from malevolent forces. These crystals held the potential for a cataclysmic event if mishandled. In response, the Culebre utilized their formidable powers to craft a cryogenic chamber, an icy sanctuary that would control the latent power within the ethereal triOsmium. With great care and precision, Hathor and the Culebre enclosed the crystals within the chamber, confining and controlling the jewels power.

Once securely stored away, the majestic dragon with Hathor on its back took flight. Its massive wings spanned the sky as it soared above the enchanting Scottish Highlands. The dragon rose through the clouds, ascending ever higher until it reached the heavens themselves. With a graceful descent, it skimmed the surface of the loch, its magnificence reflected in the shimmering waters below. Then, it left to its home in Wales.

Hathor and the Culebre planned to dwell in harmony, cherishing each blissful moment while patiently awaiting the eventual liberation that would accompany the return of the Izbek.

Amazingly, not even a day had passed when suddenly the rescue ship descended from the heavens, hovering, and shimmering in all its silvery glory above the mountain.

inviting Hathor onto its back, The Culebre transformed one last time into the magnificent dragon and took flight, soaring into the sky to finally find salvation.

CHAPTER 62

RETURNING TO NORMAL

I n the aftermath of the events that had taken place at the Loch, the waters returned to some semblance of tranquility. The cold east wind blowing in from the Moray Firth rustled the reeds along the shores and swept over the grasses and heather on the valley sides, providing a freshness in the air that perpetuated the chilling drama that had been played out in this mysterious valley.

Drumnadrochit was left smoldering and in ruins, the result of the Culebre dragons' cleansing actions against the malevolent and cannibalistic corpses remotely controlled by the microbial robots streaming through their veins.

Government investigators had arrived on the scene to make sense of how an entire village had suffered a collective psychosis. Tales of a mysterious dragon being the cause were dismissed as local superstitions akin to the monster that roamed the local waters on which this very settlement stood. Eventually, the village would be rebuilt as an exact replica of its former self, ready to greet the steady flow of tourists arriving in the hope of catching a glimpse of the Loch's most famous resident.

However, now that the Morrigan and the Boobrie had been vanquished, any sightings of that monster might never happen again. For centuries, they had haunted this mystical valley, transforming into their ethereal avatars to bathe in the moonlight from above and the magical glow of the crystals from below the loch. With their demise, they would appear no more.

Boleskine House, now vacant, awaits a brave occupant undaunted by its malevolent past. Urquhart Castle stays steadfast on the shoreline, bearing witness to another extraordinary chapter in the loch's history, keeping a silent vigil. Only whispers and rumors echo around its crumbling walls, as the ghostly howls of the wind evoke eerie sounds resembling bagpipes played by souls long departed.

David, true to his word, sought out Interpol, finding a sympathetic ear. They opened an investigation into GPI and found evidence that they had infiltrated the Sobek corporation and stolen deadly pathogens from clandestine laboratories in unregulated Central Asia. Later raids, with the help of the World Health Organization, closed them down, making them safe. The leaders of GPI, including Anja Beck, were sent to trial at the court for international justice in The Hague.

Jordan returned to London and her medical company, relieved to have prevented another, potentially more devastating global pandemic, but also with a newfound sense of responsibility. Her nanotechnology division held immense promise for future medical breakthroughs.

However, she pondered whether restricting access solely to elitist individuals who could afford the expensive treatments was the right approach. She vowed to exercise greater discernment and to strive towards making these miraculous cures accessible to the masses.

Malak left Scotland with a profound sense of self-worth.

Gaining the knowledge that elucidated the origins of his amazing abilities, he understood that he was a direct descendant of Nanuk, an ancient Izbek shapeshifter who had, to Malak's immense joy, returned to her ancestral home world. Upon his return to his office in London, he continued his mission to raise awareness about the endangered polar bears. With influential contacts at his disposal, he continued his work with renewed hope.

The Selkie made her way back to the Hebrides, precisely to the spot where her escape pod had entered the sea. It was the same place where she and the primitive people had constructed a stone circle upon her arrival. When she caught sight of the descending ship from the sky, a profound sense of relief and joy washed over her. A tubular appendage resembling a drinking straw descended from the ship, its surface covered in a mercurial liquid and dipped just below the sea's surface. Without hesitation, the Selkie swam into it and was instantly transported onboard, where she was warmly welcomed by her rescuers. Finally, after ten thousand years, she shed the confines of her earthly avatars and transformed back into her true Izbek form.

Overwhelmed with relief, a serene smile spread across her face, while her mesmerizing rose-colored eyes gleamed with joy. Countless thoughts rushed through her mind - rescue had finally arrived, and she would soon be reunited with her loved ones.

Hathor, relying on the Culebre dragon as her trusted companion, returned to Snowdonia. As the ship hovered above the magnificent mountain, Hathor and the Culebre dragon gracefully ascended to meet it. Performing an aerial display as enchanting and precise as ballet dancers floating among the clouds, the pair effortlessly entered the transportation tube hanging from the ship. Upon their return to their own kind, they underwent a transformation, reverting to their true selves. The crew of the rescue vessel watched in awe as the two illustrious and pure souls found their way back home. The collective spirits on board felt a heightened sense of connection and spirituality.

Bouda and Wepwawet had instructed the UH 1 helicopter to pick them up high above the Loch and Urquhart Castle on the

Great Glen Way. The chopper carried them back to the ship that awaited them in the North Sea. Both Izbek felt disappointed that they had failed to recover the crystals.

Though they had not seen the mortal combat between Sobek and the Morrigan, they carried a deep sense of loss, believing that Sobek had been lost.

Upon returning to Cairo, Bouda resumed his responsibilities at his metallurgical company, determined to move on from the events at the Loch. Meanwhile, Ulf Cadman in his wolf form, disappeared into the desert once again, nursing his wounds. This marked the second time he had been outmatched by the insidious child shapeshifters, and he vowed not to forget it.

Meanwhile, David, Bob, and the rest of the Squad made their way back to London, ready to enjoy the rest of their field trip with the history society. The visit to Salisbury Plain and Stonehenge held particular significance for the Squad.

As they stood before the colossal stones, their gaze wandered upwards, fixating on the stars. In that moment, a question lingered in their minds - could humanity or even themselves, one day traverse the vast expanse of space, gliding through nebulae and star clusters to visit their ancestors on Izbekia? Contemplating the possibilities, their minds brimmed with curiosity and wonder.

"Maybe One day," Sarah whispered to herself.

THE END

Continue to discover what fate holds in store for the "Quad Squad" as the Izbek return to Earth seeking vengeance, by reading:

RETRIBUTION OF FIRE

BookThree

The Descendants of the Gods Trilogy

Prologue

Before time was but a distant dream, ancient tribes listened to the land as it breathed stories into the wind. Whispers carried across the valleys and over the mountains told of sky spirits descending from the heavens. Roaming Yellowstone as animals, they conversed with the terrestrial guardians of the earth. Mighty volcanoes stood as sentinels, their fiery hearts beating in unison with the pulse of the world. Their rumblings, like ancient drumbeats, reverberated through the valley, echoing the secrets of creation and destruction. Hot springs bubbled forth, their warmth a reminder of the earth's inner fire, while geysers danced like spirits released from the depths below.

From the cracks in the earth, ethereal smoke rose, veiling the boundary between the seen and unseen. The earth spirits, ancient and powerful, awoke in times of anger, causing the very ground to tremble and quake. The fires of volcanic rebirth symbolized the eternal dance of creation and destruction, weaving a tapestry of life and death. From the ashes of devastation, new life would appear, stronger and more vibrant than before, a reminder that in every ending, there lay the seeds of a new beginning.

Chapter 1: The Wrath of Nature

As the earth trembled with an unprecedented force, Hedow felt the very core of his being shaken. The surrounding land quivered and rumbled, as if nature itself seethed with anger. Little did he know, the cave that sheltered his family teetered on the verge of a cataclysmic event, poised to alter their lives forever.

Weeks prior, wisps of smoke had curled into the sky from distant mountains. The ground beneath their feet vibrated and the once serene river from which they gathered water began to boil. These were ominous omens, heralding an impending catastrophe upon their world.

As pressure beneath the Earth's surface reached a breaking point, the volcanoes erupted with a deafening roar. Rocks and gases spewed from the fiery maw of the mountains, soaring high into the air before raining down upon the land below. Lava flowed like rivers of fire down the slopes, consuming everything in its path with unrelenting fury.

Continue reading the final book in "The Descendants of Gods Trilogy"

https://mybook.to/V91K1xP
https://www.amazon.com/dp/B0D6ZSLJ1D
https://www.amazon.co.uk/dp/B0D6ZSLJ1D
https://buy.bookfunnel.com/upkfy9icld

ABOUT THE AUTHOR

R.M. Alwyn is a writer living in Southern California. Born in Huddersfield, Yorkshire in the United Kingdom, R.M attended King James School in Almondbury and the University of Manchester. He graduated with honors before emigrating to the United States. He authored his trilogy of books initially for his children before deciding to publish them.

He writes not only to entertain but also to educate and inspire readers to investigate the world we live in, its history, and the fantastic stories told in many of its cultures.

A Humble Request

I am truly touched by your decision to read my book. Your support means the world to me and fuels my passion for writing, allowing me to delve into creating more captivating stories. If you could kindly consider leaving an honest online review of my book at the platform where you made your purchase, it would mean everything to me. Your feedback holds immense value, as it guides bookstores in deciding how to further distribute and promote my work. Your time and attention devoted to reading my book fill me with gratitude, and I genuinely hope that it brought you as much joy as it brought me while I poured my heart into it.

Books published.

Raindrops of the Gods.

Jewels beneath the Loch.

Retribution of Fire.

Offspring. The Descendants.

Website: www.quadsquadauthor.com